Love Brings You Home

Rebecca Jones

This book is a work of fiction. Names, characters, places, and incidents are the product of the author's imagination or used factitiously. Any resemblance to actual events, locales, or persons living or dead, is coincidental.

Tyndail Publishing

Copyright 2019 Rebecca Jones

Dedication

Thank you to my husband, George Jones, who was patient while I escaped for hours at a time to write in my home office. Thanks to Kandice Antwine who is my friend and photographer for this project. Thanks to Republican State House Representative Pat McElraft who worked on legislation to help the 'farmers of the sea' here in Carteret County. Although this book is fiction and the names, characters, places, and incidents are the product of my imagination or used factitiously, the part about the work that Pat McElfrat has done was real. Any other resemblance to actual events, locales, or persons living or dead, is coincidental.

May this book be a spotlight on the Eastern part of North Carolina and to show awareness of the importance of how commercial fishing is to our State. This book is also about relationships and commitment; moving forward and forgiving. I hope something in this book makes you think and grow.

Chapter 1

Katlynn placed her hands on the mahogany desk and pushed the brown leather chair back toward the wall. She stood and sauntered around the desk toward the window, pulling the blinds all the way to the top. Her office was on the 18th floor. From the window she could see other tall buildings that seemed to be joined together in the New York City skyline. Cars and people below looked like ants scurrying around. Feeling a little dizzy from looking down she turned back toward her desk. A sleek chrome name plate, *Katlynn Harcourt, Editor in Chief,* stood perfectly in place on her desk. She was 35 years old; one of the youngest to advance to this title in her field of journalism.

Looking around the room her eyes stopped on the paintings Roger, the building superintendent, just hung. Of course, they were all reproductions. The first one in the row on the wall was Royal Red and Blue; a reproduction of Mark Rothko's royal blue and red squares on a canvas. The original hangs in the Art Institute in Chicago. The one next to that was A Sunday Afternoon on the Island of La Grande Jatte, by George Suerat showing a relaxed atmosphere of people on a lazy Sunday afternoon in an island. Next was Café Terrace at Night by

Vincent Van Gogh; a simple dinner café along a street. The fourth one was <u>La Moulin de la Galette</u> by Renoir of a vivid description of city life.

She had asked Roger to place a hanger on the wall, leaving an empty space. He looked confused as that was all the paintings on his work order to hang. Katlynn told him she may hang something from home. He shook his head as he closed her office door. All those paintings had lots of colors and definitely artsy like New York. Some of which she would not have chosen for her office; although very famous and nice.

Stepping back to take a look at the wall Katlynn saw her reflection in the windows. Her hair used to be mousey brown and long. Now she had short blonde hair cut into a bob that layered toward her face or she could tuck behind her ears. She really liked this cut. It showed her high cheekbones and the dimple in her right cheek when she smiled. The bangs were feathered just so. She almost did not recognize herself. She had lost weight; not intentionally, making a note to self to buy some clothes that fit.

Opening her wallet, she pulled out a picture of her and her daddy when she was 12 years old. He stood on his boat holding a shrimp net in one hand and her hand in the other. Lean and weather-worn from a lifetime on the water he had more wrinkles than she remembered. His white shrimping boots were no longer bright white; more noticeable against his dark blue jeans. He seemed to smile all over. That was the only picture she had of her childhood. She had looked into having it blown up into a poster size photo but had not been willing yet to take the chance of something happening to it. She was closer to letting it go than she had ever before, hoping to turn it into something beautiful.

She had been born in Harkers Island, North Carolina and lived there until she was 12. Among the most vivid memories of her childhood were the days she spent with her daddy when he would come back to shore after a long day out shrimping. He left early in the morning while it was still dark and would return at sunset. Katlynn remembered well her old dog Rascal would bark and jump off the porch, heading to the backyard which was the intercoastal waterway. She followed, slamming the screen door. Her mama would always yell, "Do you have to slam the door every time?" But she was long gone to answer her. Rascal always beat her to the boat.

Her daddy, Uncle Bobby and Joshua, a 20-year-old cousin worked the boat with him. Her granddaddy owned the boat; he was now in a nursing home slumped in a chair sleeping most days. Her granddaddy's daddy had owned a boat like it. Shrimping had been in the family for generations. The business handed down to the next generation of men; her daddy emphasizing that this was "man's work" and too hard on the body for his girl. She rolled her eyes.

After dinner they walked out to the dock to see the moon rise over the water as it cast a bright light in the shadows. "Maybe one day you can learn the business, Sweet Pea. With all the new regulations the government is handing out we will need someone like you to write all those letters and talk to the officials that are trying to change things. All I know is how to shrimp," he said with a sigh.

She loved sitting on the dock looking at the boat with all its cables and wenches, nets put away and cleaned for the night. He loved it too. For as long as she could remember he wanted her to know the many types and species found in the North Carolina waters. North Carolina has three main types of shrimp: brown, pink and white. They live in marshes and estuaries when they are very young because it is safe there. When they are fully grown, they swim out of the estuaries and into the ocean. Shrimp are an annual crop. The amount varies from year to year of how much is caught depending on the weather. If it is a very cold winter, then it will be a small population in the spring.

Her mama hated living in Harkers Island; she hated the house they lived in (which originally belonged to her daddy's great granddaddy.) That was no secret. Her mama and daddy had met at Duke University in Durham, North Carolina. He was a biology major and graduated with honors. Her mama was an education major. His family was from Harkers Island and hers was from Wake Forest, North Carolina. They came from two very different backgrounds, but were madly in love. Her mama's family had warned her not to marry him. Her grandmother had said, "The boy has salt water for blood. He cannot stay away from it. You will see. Then you will be stuck in time, eking out a living; you know- barely existing with difficulty and effort." They married shortly after graduation and they proved them wrong. He took a job with the government in Raleigh, North Carolina at the Capitol Building overseeing the North Carolina Environmental Quality department. She found a job teaching at the high school. Life was wonderful until granddaddy "took sick" and he moved her to Harkers Island to take over the family shrimping business. It was supposed to be for only a little while until he got back on his feet, but that did not happen. A year later Katlynn was born and her parents never left. Her mama said the house looked like it did the day she moved in. Her mama was right. They lived on the water, which was beautiful and calming, but eking out a living was what everyone did. No updating houses with paint and fancy furniture.

"Your teacher told your mama today that you have a gift for writing. Your mama has a gift too, but she has not used it in years. She quit teaching and works two jobs waitressing. I told her she does not have to do that now that the business has had two good years, but she won't quit." He shifted to stretch his legs. She could remember that night like it was yesterday. He had been telling her that she needed to be a writer "because you have something important to share." He said that again and again.

Two days later the nightly TV news showed an enormous hurricane heading right toward their little island. Her daddy packed two suitcases; one for her and one for her mama and was waiting at the diner when her mama got off work. "I am taking you and Katlynn inland to Wake Forest. Your sister is expecting you. We have been told to evacuate tonight. Rascal is staying with me as your sister said her two cats did not like dogs." Being 12 years old she had no idea what all that meant. They drove through the night and at sunlight arrived inland. Mama waved goodbye to daddy, kissing him on his cheek. He stuck the photo into Katlynn's hand. "Isn't daddy and Rascal staying with us?" She asked as she watched him back out the driveway and out of sight. "No," mama said, "your daddy will stay with that blame old boat and old house." Under her breath she wondered out loud, "I do not know if it will stand." She left the room and started putting the clothes away in the drawers as if they were staying for a long, long time.

And they did stay for a long, long time. The hurricane came through and wiped out the house like the story of the big bad wolf where it huffed and puffed and blew the house down. Her daddy and Rascal were in the shrimping boat when it became unmoored and tossed like confetti in the ocean. He was found three days later lying dead on the shore 10 miles away. His death hurt her so. Writing did become a way for Katlynn to grapple with loss and to transform it into art over despair. One must look closely at the world, gathering gifts of experience and those things that one might need to keep to shore up against uncertain futures like the loss that came. Looking back now she can see that hers were days of wonder and days of

12

fleeting happiness and her unquestioning belief that her life would always be just as it was then.

They never went back to Harkers Island. Her Aunt Sophia had her daddy's body brought to Wake Forest to be buried in her church's graveyard. The day of the funeral was a day of steady rain. Grief sounded like a roar like that of an ocean held inside a seashell. After the funeral she ran to her room and stayed there for two days. But life must go on. She now had a room of her own and lived in big house with her Aunt Sophia, her mama and two cats. A white picket fence surrounded the yard; a sidewalk and park nearby and lots of new friends had her settle into a new life. She fastened herself somewhere else; being moored into new beginnings. Children bounce back better than adults she has always been told.

But her mama had bounced back, too quickly, she thought. Her mama took the teaching exam to be licensed and started teaching at the local community college. Maggie had moved on. This made Katlynn furious on one hand, but on the other one she had not seen her mama so happy. Aunt Sophia asked her every Sunday to go to church but she refused. She was still mad at God. How could God take her daddy and her life as she knew it away? Just like that, as she snapped her fingers. She watched her Aunt Sophia and her mama walk across the street to church every Sunday morning at 11:00 a.m. They did not pressure her into going.

So, Katlynn threw herself into her studies and after school clubs. After high school she chose to go to Syracuse University to study journalism and to get away from North Carolina as fast as she could. She took summer jobs in New York so that she would not have to come back home. She landed jobs in the Chicago area to gain experience and now she had "arrived" in her new office in New York City.

Her daddy would be proud. She was like the shrimp; growing up in the safe marshes and now that she was grown, she had swum out into the big ocean into the world.

Chapter 2

Maggie pulled her car up to the curb and put it in park. A big red SOLD sign had been placed diagonally on the For Sale sign at 100 Willow Tree Lane. She was waiting for her realtor to do a final walk through before the closing on her house. She and Jim had dreamed of living in this house when they were young and still lived inland. The house was one and a half story with a large front porch and fenced in backyard. It would have been wonderful for Katlynn to have grown up there. How ironic that 20 years later she was moving into this house.

Katlynn was the same age as she was when Jim had died in the storm. A widow at 35 years old with a 12-year-old. If it had not been for Sophia taking over and being the rock, she would not have made it, she thought. Oh, it was hard on Katlynn, but children are resilient. She, on the other hand, had pretended to move on. She filled her days at the community college teaching GED classes and a couple of evenings a week taking an Art Class. She missed Jim every day of her life. She just handled the grief in a different way than Katlynn. She wondered if Katlynn really dealt with her grief. Maggie knew that Katlynn blamed her for not talking Jim into staying inland, but no one could talk him into it. Not even his uncles who left for safety. She could not figure out how the draw to the water and shrimping could consume him. How could he put that in first place over her and Katlynn? She was still trying to figure that one out.

Maybe Katlynn was right. Maybe she should have begged and cried and pleaded for him to stay. Her parents were right in the end. He did have salt water in his blood. Maggie had not provided a happy childhood for her daughter. She had been so angry that Jim would not move back to the life she had imagined they would have that she "punished" him by staying away from that house. At first, she took the waitress job to get out of the house for a few hours per day. Then they had some

16

years where the weather didn't cooperate. She had to work two jobs to put food on the table. When Jim did have a good year, she was so used to being gone away from him and that house, someone else's house, that it became her norm.

Someone else's house. That is what she called it. It never did seem like home to her. The house was furnished with all of Jim's family's things. Even the pictures on the wall were part of them, not her. She suggested that they paint the walls at least some bright colors. She had even brought paint samples home from the Ace Hardware so that Jim could help decide. She remembered the confused look on his face when he saw the samples. The house looked just fine to him; a home that said *comfort* to him. The one he remembered his daddy and his granddaddy and happy memories in. So, she threw the samples in the trash and never mentioned it again.

Even when she found out she was pregnant with Katlynn the 'nesting' began to stir in her. The spare bedroom, if you could call it that, was filled with papers and files for the shrimping business. There was even a small desk with a lamp on it next to the window. When she asked Jim about where he could put all that stuff to make room for the baby, he had that look again. Move it? Where? It had always been that way. So, she found a crib at a yard sale, painted it herself and shoved it in the corner of the room. Some nursery. Not what she had imagined.

Her realtor beeped her horn as she pulled in behind her and startled her. Maggie greeted her and walked up to the front door. Mary handed her the keys. "This is your house. Let's go in." Maggie turned the key and opened the door. The living room had built-in bookcases beside the large fireplace which was painted white. The walls were painted in a light teal accenting the fireplace. An island separated the kitchen from the living space. A built-in table with bench seats were in an alcove lined with pillows that matched the living room walls. The two bedrooms were on the right side of the house separated by a Jack and Jill bathroom. A gazebo was in the back corner of the backyard. It was the perfect house for her. She loved the front porch. She would buy a bench for it soon.

Maybe Katlynn would join her and Sophia for Thanksgiving this year. She talked to her daughter at least once a week, but had not seen her since Katlynn went away to college. She made excuses for why she could not come. Most years she was on a writing assignment, sometimes out of the country. It amazed her how unlucky she was to have to work all the holidays. In her heart she knew that Katlynn probably volunteered.

Oh, she could put the blame on herself as well. Not once did she travel to New York to see her. Sophia had flown there to see the Macy's Day Parade just last year. Maggie had made an excuse that she thought she had the Flu. Maybe the guilt she felt deep inside kept her from dealing with the decisions she had made. A guilty conscience is an open wound only TRUTH can heal. And the truth was that maybe if she had made an effort to attempt to be happy in Harkers Island things would be different. A true relationship is someone who accepts your past, supports your present and loves you and encourages your future. She had not been that for Jim. They were supposed to be there for a short time; not a lifetime. But then should he have bent for her as well? She was after all the other part of this relationship. In the end he was worth her tears, worth her laughter and worth her heart.

Maybe that was why she was drawn to this house on Willow Tree Lane. The tree is known for its roots which are remarkable for their toughness, size and tenacity to live. Maybe she had missed it altogether. The people of Harkers Island are a persistence, determined and perseverance folk. Tenacity is the ability to hang on when letting go appears most attractive. Maybe, just maybe, Jim stayed through the storm to not only protect the family business, but to protect a lifestyle. And yet maybe he was afraid of change as it leads to a new beginning.

Maggie was excited and anxious to set her roots into this house. She was tired of focusing all of her energy into fighting the old. It was time for her to build the new; to close her eyes to old ends and open her heart to a new beginning.

The papers were signed and the moving truck pulled into the driveway. Sophia and their friends helped unload the boxes and placed the furniture in its proper places. They all left and she was alone in the house for the first time that night. It felt like home. It would be days before everything was unboxed and put away, but for the first time in a long time she felt settled and happy.

Chapter 3

The alarm on her cell phone startled Katlynn. She had set it to remind her of the meetings with her staff. Four out of the five of them had been on assignment and were back to report to her their findings for next month's magazine.

Her first appointment was with Cameron. He was small in stature for a man, with bright orange curly hair. He had been on assignment of visiting the area Homeless Shelters. Cameron had not only visited the shelters, but had gone out with the local police for the annual homeless count. He had actually tried to spend a week out in one of the camps, but only made it for two nights.

A good journalist asks "why" as they gather facts. He reported a lack of affordable housing and the limited scale of housing assistance have contributed to the current housing crisis and to homelessness. One of the biggest links are poor people are stuck in poverty and feel they cannot get out. Lack of education and lack of employment opportunities remain high. But the major factors he found were addiction, mental illness, and domestic violence. Those seemed to resonate more than anything.

Katlynn shifted in her chair and leaned a little toward him. "Great facts, Cameron, but where is the story?"

Cameron sat up a little straighter and smiled. "Katlynn, when I tried to live out in the streets, I found out a lot about myself. One thing I found out was that it takes a strong person to live out there. I had left all my money at home; I had begged with a sign on the side of the road with only collecting $5.00 for the day. People passed me by and some jeered at me. A real homeless man came and took me to the Salvation Army for a free meal. That is where I met Randy."

"Randy is the manager over the meal and nightly stay division of the Salvation Army. After a hot meal he showed us where we would bed down for the night. When all was settled in that is when I found him in the office and told him who I was. I asked him for an interview. Randy told me once he had a job as a manager over a retail store. That store went bankrupt and he was laid off. Around that time, he had a heart attack while unemployed with no insurance and no job. He lost everything he had ever worked for. In his depression he began to drink and do drugs. His wife left him and took the children. He said he hopped a train to another state and lived on the streets for a couple of years."

"Randy said on Christmas Eve he sat outside a large church and watched as people all dressed up went inside for the service. After they all were inside and the doors were closed, he said he sat under a bush right outside the window to listen to the music. He heard the story of Jesus and he realized he had hit rock bottom. But that rock bottom became a foundation on which he rebuilt his life. Someone on the security team at church found him in the bushes and asked him to come in. He sat on the last row, had a meal with the members after the service and they took him to a shelter."

"There he was asked if he wanted help to get back on his feet or just a hot meal for the night. Randy said he cried like a baby and asked for help for a future. It was a long process. He was addicted to alcohol and drugs, had low self-esteem and no job."

Cameron said he asked Randy what one thing he would like to tell him in one sentence.

Katlynn sat back in her chair to listen.

"When we hit the lowest point, we are open to change."

Katlynn let out a sigh. How true. And now Randy had a good paying job, a place to live and a purpose. No, he did not get his family back, as they had moved on and were happy. He had to accept what is, let go of what was, and have faith in what will be.

Cameron waited for Katlynn's response.

"Cameron, you did an excellent job! Put all that together and write me that story. I need it by the end of the week."

After he left Katlynn began to reflect on the story. Randy had renewed his faith and moved forward. She was still mad at God for taking her daddy and her life as she knew it. She was still mad at her mama, too. But somehow a soft spot was forming in her heart.

Her next appointment was with Lindsay. Lindsay was a tall, lean natural blonde with shoulder length hair. She was the youngest of her employees; just 22 years old fresh out of college. A true blonde, tanned California girl, she wanted the assignment of investigating if tanning booths or even sun tanning causes cancer. Since her move to New York she had visited the tanning booths since the lack of sunny beaches were not there.

Lindsay came into the office and was too nervous to sit down. She had her portfolio open and was walking around the room.

Katlynn let her pace and she came around to the front of her desk and leaned up against it.

"OMG, Katlynn. I had no idea! Since moving to New York, I visit the tanning booth at least twice a week. At first it was just once a month. I found out in my research that the connection between UV radiation and melanoma is clear. And I also found out that it is addictive. At first, I was skeptical. Then I tried for the last month to not go to the tanning booth. But I found out I could not keep away. The researchers are right. They say that UV light has been shown to increase the release of endorphins, the feel-good chemicals that relieve pain and generate the feelings of well-being. They say this leads to dependency."

"The doctors say as many as 90% of melanomas are estimated to be caused by ultraviolet exposure. It is good to be outside in the sun for short bursts, but not to lay out all day, and especially you get a better (or should I say worse) dose of it laying in a tanning booth."

Katlynn came over to her and laid a hand on her shoulder.

"Did the doctor you interviewed give you some suggestions or alternatives?"

Lindsay responded, "Yes, that over-the-counter sunless tanning creams and lotions may be an option for those who want to have tanned skin while avoiding health risks of UV exposure and inhaled and absorbed DHA."

Katlynn asked her what was the one sentence that she could define should be the take away from this research.

Lindsay sat down in the chair, her hands in her lap and said, "That he encourages people to embrace and value the skin in which they were born."

Katlynn looked at Lindsay and smiled. "So, take the doctor's advice. But I encourage you to make an appointment with a dermatologist just to be sure you are okay."

Lindsay left the office and Katlynn remembered something her daddy had said to her when she was 8 years old.

"Sweet Pea, I want you to always remember this quote by Ralph Waldo Emerson. 'To be yourself in a world that is constantly trying to make you something else is the greatest accomplishment.' Do not forget that."

At the time she had no idea what he was talking about, but looking back she realized that her daddy was a true Harkers Island fisherman; he could not or would not have been happy in an office sitting in Raleigh with a shirt and tie on. Why could her mother not see that?

Damian came through the door whistling. He was a full-blooded Italian man with dark hair and an accent, even though he had been born in America. He was raised by his grandmother who had come over from the old country as she liked to say.

"I just got back from a farm to table place in New Hampshire and we must go there for Thanksgiving. You don't have a family and neither do I, so that settles it," he said as he came through the door and sat sideways in the leather chair in the corner, his lanky legs hanging over the sides of the chair arms.

Katlynn smiled and shook her head. He was so full of life and adventure.

"Okay, tell me about this place. When did Italians from Italy start celebrating Thanksgiving, you know, a traditional American holiday?" She said this jokingly of course.

"La signorina, you know nothing," he said teasingly. "I shall educate you. My grandmother celebrated La Festa del Ringraziamento every year. It is actually a Festival of Thanks which refers to a variety of religious holidays held throughout the year to honor patron saints. As I was driving around New Hampshire looking for a story for you I happened to fall upon a farm which had a large red barn and a sign that said Farm to Table House. It intrigued me so I decided to check it out. It seems that three times a year this family opens their farm up for a meal. There is a long waiting list and a pretty hefty price to get to come. A long set of wooden tables and chairs are set up on the barn floor. Only 55 people can attend."

Damian now had Katlynn's interest. "So, what is on the menu? I thought Italy did not have turkeys."

"Oh, they do not have turkeys. It is much different than America's meal. Of course, you have to start out with a white wine served with a Ricotta stuffed mushrooms and baked seasoned olives as an appetizer. The first course is a roasted pumpkin and pear soup. The main dish is a roast lamb. Side dishes are fennel in Bechamel sauce with Parmesan Cheese, Rosemary roasted potatoes, and Sweet and Sour Roasted beets and onions. Dessert is Tiramisu or a Chocolate Chestnut Cake."

"Oh my, how my mouth is watering already."

"So, Katlynn, with me being my charming irresistible self I was shown the menu and the barn where the meal is served and all the decorations they will have on the tables and wait, wait for it! I secured two invitations for us as I kind of threw your name around." Damian waited for her response.

"I like it, but it is like we are doing an advertisement for them. That is not what this is about. You know how I like stories. It tells of the souls of people." Katlynn watched as Damian sat up straight in the chair and moved closer to her. He looked serious for the first time she had known him.

Damian's shoulders drooped and he had a sadness about him. "My parents died in a car wreck when I was four years old. I cannot remember them. But my grandmother took me in her home and every Sunday and all the holidays were spent with family; you know, aunts, uncles, cousins and even neighbors."

"You can say that Italian family life can be characterized by loyalty and closeness. From the immediate nuclear family to more extended relatives, they remain close as a unit through several generations. Large dinners are the center of it all. Even though migration with some families geographically separated, the family is still the center of the social structure providing unity and stability. That is why this Farm to Table House does this every year; because her Italian family has all died, she is extending it to others." Damian put his head in his hands and then looked up at Katlynn.

"I understand. Did you get some good pictures while you were there?"

He smiled and turned on the iPod for her to see. It was a beautiful place. She could see why he fell in love with it all and how he was drawn to it.

"What is the one thing she said that you took away to learn from?"

Damian thought for a moment and said, "She said family is like branches on a tree. We all grow different directions yet our roots remain as one."

Damian stood to leave. He turned around at the door and said, "Katlynn, there was a sign that hung above the head chair of the table. It said – 'Family ties are precious threads no matter where we roam. They draw us close to those we love and pull our hearts to home.' Think about going with me to Thanksgiving dinner. I have two tickets, you know?"

He shut the door quietly as he left. Katlynn went over to the window and pulled the blinds down, darkening the room. Her next appointment would be after lunch and she was getting hungry. Or was it the knot in her stomach when Damian talked about family. Family. Her 'perfect' world had crumbled when her daddy died. Her mama tried to help her with her grief, but looking back her mama was dealing with her own grief and guilt. There must not have been much left of her own self, much less anything to give Katlynn. She remembers that day her mama dropped her off to college like it was yesterday. She kissed her on the cheek and handed her an envelope. She had stuffed that envelope in a drawer and had not opened it for the whole four years of college. When she packed her dorm room to leave after graduation, she found it and opened it.

It read, "To my daughter. Never forget that I love you. Life is filled with hard times and good times. Learn from everything you can. Be the woman I know you can be. Love Mom."

With this thought Katlynn rode the elevator down 18 floors and walked out into the sunshine to grab some lunch.

Chapter 4

Maggie placed the stripped pillows on the bench and then watered the yellow mums she had sitting on each step leading up to the front porch. She had put the finishing touches on the house and stepped back to take a look.

Beautiful, she thought, and very inviting. Contentment. That is what she was experiencing for the first time in a long time. She thought back to when she was younger; a new wife and a young mother. She remembered thinking "if I lose weight, get a better job, move to another town, then I would be happy. If I saved money or took a cruise to a beautiful tropical island then I would be satisfied. If I got married and had a kid, I would be content. I need to do all these things in order to get happy with my life."

But she was always looking for something else. Now that she had done some soul searching, she came to some new knowledge. In order to be happy, she had learned to be thankful for everything she has now; for the food on her table and this beautiful home to sleep in at night. She learned to live in the moment. She had to forget about the past. Not that she would ever forget Jim, but to forget the bad parts that she could no longer change. She learned to not worry about things that have not happened yet, too. Maggie learned to follow her dreams and passions. Jim was gone and would not come back. She had learned to strive for the best and settle for whatever she ended up with. But most importantly she had learned to love herself for who she was. She learned she did not have to change anything about herself in order to be happy and content. She learned that she did not need a man to complete her. She was complete in her own skin.

Maggie wondered if Katlynn would like her; if they could be friends. Mother-daughter relationships are complex and diverse. They talked at least once a week, but it was mostly about the weather or surface level stuff about their jobs. She used to have this idealistic expectation about their relationship;

that they would tell each other their most inner thoughts and be best buddies. There was not really conflict in their relationship; it was more of she did not know her child.

Maybe she would call her and ask for forgiveness for the mistakes that she made in the past. Did she do things that scarred Katlynn for life?

Sophia knocked on the door and waited for Maggie to answer. Maggie finally made it to the door and invited her in.

Sophia looked at her sister and took her by her hand to the kitchen. She made them both a cup of coffee and handed it to Maggie.

"I know that look. What in the world is it now? You have this beautiful home and life. Why the sad look?" Sophia sat across from her to see her reactions.

"Oh, I was just thinking about Katlynn. She calls me every Wednesday night and fills me in on her work. But I have not seen her in years. What am I doing wrong?" Maggie took a sip of the coffee and blew to cool it.

"Maggie, to move away from your parents and live your own life is normal. You did it. I did it. To keep in touch once a week for many daughters works perfectly well. It can be a sign that the relationship is strong and can tolerate distance. But you may want to call her once in a while. She always does the calling doesn't she?"

"Yes. I know it is guilt on my part. Maybe I will host a Thanksgiving Dinner at my home this year and invite her. What if she says no?" Maggie hung her head down.

"What if she says 'yes'? Maggie, it is time you laid that burden down and surrender your pride. Surrendering is not about giving up, it is about letting go."

Sophia put her coffee mug in the sink and handed Maggie the phone.

Maggie dialed Katlynn's number and listened to it ring; she picked up on the fourth ring.

"Hi mama! Is everything okay? You never call," Katlynn said without thinking how that sounded.

"Yes, I just was thinking of you and was wondering what you were up to. I have all the boxes gone and even have flowers and pillows on the front porch. It looks like home." Maggie waited for her reply.

"I would love to see it mama; send me pictures."

"I was hoping you could hop a plane and come to Wake Forest. I could pick you up at the Raleigh airport. Do you get off at Thanksgiving? Maybe we could have a traditional meal here with some neighbors."

Katlynn thought about that for a moment and ask, "Isn't Aunt Sophia going to be around?"

"Oh, she is going to take a trip to Paris over the holidays. She will be home before Christmas." Maggie was feeling a little bummed.

"Let me make some phone calls and I will get back to you on that one, mama." Katlynn told her about the findings of the skin cancer that Lindsay had discovered and wrote about. "Do you think daddy had that? Or for that matter all of that side of the family in Harkers Island?"

Maggie answered that question quickly. "Probably, but do you think you could get those folks to see a doctor? I think no way they would entertain such."

Katlynn asked, "Mama, do you ever hear from that side of the family?"

Maggie paused before answering. "No dear. I have not heard from anyone in years."

"Why is that?" Katlynn wished she had not just asked that question. She was not ready for an answer and it sounded like she was attacking her mama, but that is not what she meant.

Maggie was silent for what seemed like minutes. Katlynn thought she had hit a nerve with her or had hung up.

Maggie took a deep breath and began. "Katlynn, it is my fault. I have been dealing with this for years. I hated that place, and our life there and when Jim died, I did not want to ever look back when we left. Between anger and guilt and hurt I let Sophia take over. I was not able to deal; was not strong enough. I should have buried him in Harkers Island instead of here in Wake Forest. His family was hurt and angry with me and I abandoned them at a time when we should have embraced. I cannot change that now. Done is done."

Katlynn had not thought of how it must have made her daddy's family feel that they had left until now. Being a young child, she had assumed that when one parent dies you move and make a new life and that side of the family is gone. It had never occurred to her that they were still her family. But then did they ever try to contact her and her mama?

Maggie continued. "I have thought about it recently to see if I can find how to contact any of them. I am afraid, Katlynn.

Afraid that they will not talk to me or worse abandon me. I took your daddy's jacket when he left us that night in Wake Forest. I know he probably needed that coat, but I wanted something of him. I slept with it for months because it had his smell. Then one day it lost the smell."

Maggie began to cry soft sobs and Katlynn's heart went out to her mama.

"I did not know that. Do you still have that jacket?"

"No, it lost its smell about the same time that I received my teaching license back and got the job as a professor at the community college. I took that as a sign to let it go. So, I took it to the American Red Cross and handed it to a lady. When I was about to leave the lady ran to the door and put a piece of paper in my hand."

"What was it? What did it say?" Katlynn was curious now.

"You must have gotten your writing ability from your daddy. It was a quote he wrote. 'You must not abandon ship in a storm.' And he had another quote by Vincent Van Gogh."

Katlynn thought for a moment and said, "By Vincent Van Gogh? I thought he only painted."

Maggie laughed. "Yes, the quote was 'The fisherman know that the sea is dangerous and the storm terrible, but they have never found these dangers sufficient reason for remaining ashore.'"

"Wow. Lots of double meanings. Do you still have those papers he wrote or did you get rid of that too?" Katlynn wondered out loud.

Maggie was hurt because of this accusation. But then she had not proved herself worthy of her daughter's trust all these years. "Yes, I have it. I will always have it. I can show them to you sometime when we see each other. Which I hope will not be too long."

Katlynn told her mama goodbye and that she loved her and would call her on Wednesday.

When Maggie hung up, she went out to the porch and sat. She did her best thinking while on that bench. Maybe we should not abandon ship every time we encounter a storm in our life. A smooth sea never made a good sailor. One thing was certain. When Maggie came out of the storm, she was not the same person who walked in. That is the beauty of a storm.

Chapter 5

Katlynn pushed the 'walk' button on the street post and waited for the light to change to cross the street. She was in the mood for some chili and a grilled cheese sandwich. Something warm on this cool autumn day. Winter would be coming soon to New York. She did not like the cold, bitter, snowy winters. This was the time of year she longed for North Carolina. Harkers Island had its share of bad weather – cold rainy days in the winter, flooding on the streets and wind; even tornados and sometimes hurricanes. She shuddered at the word 'hurricane.' Maybe it was the sunny days that seemed to linger into the night that she remembered. The carefree days and lack of responsibility of a child. Yes, that was what she was longing for.

She longed for the enchanted place of her childhood. She remembered how she and Rascal sat on the dock, toes dipping into the water at high tide. Yet at low tide the water looked far away. She had learned in school about the moon and its gravitational pull and how it worked scientifically, yet it still was a mystery to her. The ocean had its own rhythm and no one could escape or change it.

She remembered the thick, humid air cut with the salty smell at low tide. At low tide Rascal would jump off the dock and go for a swim. She remembered laughing so hard at him. She loved the high tide and her dog loved the low tide. They had such differences and yet loved each other – as best friends.

She also remembered moving inland to live with Aunt Sophia. Katlynn was almost a teenager by then. She was ready for people friends. She learned to love her new life; there were much more opportunities for her. Looking back, she could see why her mama wanted her to grow up in Wake Forest instead of Harkers Island. But both had shaped her life. She was grateful for both.

The waitress interrupted her thoughts to take her order.

"Water with lemon, please. I would like chili and a grilled cheese sandwich, also." Katlynn placed her hand over her heart. She wanted a hot cup of tea, but her heart murmur had been active lately. Or at least that was what she hoped it was. She was trying to lay off the caffeine to see if that helped. If not, she would make that appointment to see the doctor. She had not been to a doctor in years. She had lost a lot of weight recently thinking if she ignored it, whatever it was, would go away.

She had been ignoring little things all her life. Things like not dealing with her feelings about her mama. Or for that matter not dealing with her disappointment of not having her daddy around for him to cheer her on. Or maybe the feelings of hurt, grief that she chose to hold on to and to hold against the people she loved who were left. Maybe her heart hurt not because of a physical ailment, but because she had been ignoring little problems which compounded into something bigger. Nobody likes conflict, but sweeping issues under the rug ultimately causes more damage than addressing things directly.

But today she and her mama actually had a real conversation; one that adults had – not mama and child. Maybe she would think about going home to North Carolina for Thanksgiving.

Looking at her watch she had 15 minutes before her next appointment. She paid her bill, left a tip on the table and walked back to her office.

When she was a field journalist, she was given an assignment and had to adhere to it. She never did like that as she always found a 'better' story, but was not allowed to follow it. Therefore, since she was now the Editor in Chief her style of management worked well. Well, with most of her employees. She never knew what Hannah would come up with. Hannah was a free spirit. If she would have been born in a different time, she would have been a great hippie. She was a small woman, wore natural fibers and organic materials only. Most of her employees checked in with her everyday as to their progress. Not so with Hannah. She had not heard from her for a week. Her cell phone must have been out of range because she could not leave a message for her either. She had no idea what Hannah had been up to.

Hannah knocked on the door, but did not wait for Katlynn to answer it. She came into the office at almost a run and stopped short of running into her.

"Slow down! What happened to you? You are filthy dirty. Here, let me put something down over the chair for you to sit on." Katlynn found a throw in the closet and slung it over the chair.

"I came right here to report," Hannah said as she saluted her like a soldier.

"You could have gone home to bathe. You look like you have been living in a mud puddle. What have you been doing for this whole week? And I tried to reach you, but you did not answer. You know we have had this conversation before that you need to check in with me." Katlynn was a little irritated.

"Spelunking. You cannot take a cell phone there. You wear the least amount of clothes to be decent in and take nothing with you. I stumbled across a group of spelunkers when I was hiking. I was going to write about eating wild plants; you know, what is not poison and how to tell. But they invited me to come along so I went." Hannah brushed her hair with her hand and a small clump of dirt fell out.

"Spelunking. What kind of story can you glean from that? Other than a vacation guide in which I do not pay for you to go on vacations." Katlynn handed her a tissue to put the dirt in.

"Before you get all huffy can I at least tell you about it?" Hannah said defensively.

"Ok, here goes. I was hiking and came along this group of people, about 5 of them, who asked me if I had ever gone into a real cave. I had not so they asked me to come along. First, we zip lined to the bottom of this hill. Then we crawled on our hands and knees into the side of the mountain cave. At one point I was lying on my back and swam through a hole no wider than an MRI machine with the cave ceiling a few inches from my face. Yes, it was a lot of fun! If you are claustrophobic this would not be for you. It was invigorating. The experience was incredibly rewarding. There were magical sights, thousands of years in the making, sculpted rocks and the delicate formations were a joy to behold."

Katlynn stood up and stretched, her expression was one of disappointment.

Hannah continued. "We learned about using safety equipment, such as a helmet and headlamp, properly decontaminating your gear and improving techniques so that everyone can learn to cave safely. We stayed for a whole week in there. The bright light of the day hurt our eyes when we finally emerged outside." Hannah wiped her face with the back of her hand and looked to see how dirty it was.

Katlynn came over to her and bent down. "It looks like you had a nice vacation. Go home and shower and then we can talk about it. Your review is tomorrow."

Hannah pushed herself back into the chair to get some space.

"Katlynn, I do have a story in all this. I want to explain. I know it looks like I have been out having fun; although I did, it was with purpose."

"Ken was the leader. The other four people were recovering drug addicts. They all had gone through the detox program and their bodies were clean from the drugs. However, this whole experience was a metaphor for surviving. The safety equipment meant to remember how to protect yourself from danger of returning to bad behaviors. The helmet meant to protect your mental capacity. The headlamp represents the reflectors. The proper decontamination means the neutralization and removal of dangerous substances. Improving yourself is a self-reformation. "

Katlynn stepped back and pulled up a chair. She had never been spelunking before nor did she have a desire to go, but she did see how that fit into life. Everyone has a story of survival; very different stories, but stories just the same.

Hannah continued. "Like I said before, at one time the ceiling of the cave was inches from my face. I could smell the dirt and feel the coolness of the water drip on me. I almost began to panic but Ken told us to breathe and keep pushing and pulling until we came to the larger opening. When I pushed my shoulders through the last tight place, I was hurting a little, but once I was freed it felt so good to sit up and stretch. We all high fived each other. Ken told us a story. He ended it by saying 'just when the caterpillar thought his world was over, he became a butterfly.' Then we went out into the light."

Katlynn smiled as she watched the excitement in Hannah's eyes.

"We then had to adjust our eyes and get our bearings. As we began our hike again down the mountain back to camp Ken said something so profound." Hannah sat up a little straighter and looked very serious.

"He said, 'Walk on, out of the darkness' and no one said a word until we got back to camp."

Katlynn shook her head in agreement. Hannah told her she could write the story and get it to her tomorrow along with great pictures. And that is why, thought Katlynn, that I let my employees have leeway with their work.

Katlynn walked over to the window and looked outside at the graying sky. Rain was in the forecast again. Darkness. A random memory came to her. She was 13 years old; Aunt Sophia and her mama had requested that she go to the Christmas Eve church service. She went because it was Christmas and they asked her to, but she reminded them that it did not mean she would go on Sunday mornings. She was still mad at God, she told them. However, that night the ushers turned all the lights off in the church and they were in darkness. She remembered feeling around for her mama's hand. A woman came into the church with a single lighted candle. She began to pass out all the candles, lighting each one, to everyone in the church. All of a sudden, the light was so warm and bright. It had warmed her heart she had to admit.

Then another memory came to her mind. She remembered the day her daddy and mama took her to Beaufort, NC to see the Flotilla. She remembered that was a funny word. Her daddy explained it was a boat parade. She felt warm and safe sitting between her parents as the Christmas lights reflected over the water.

All of a sudden Kaylynn had that feeling of tightness in her chest again. The feeling of sadness and memories and nostalgia. She rang her assistant's desk and asked her to come in. Ella came rushing in to find that Katlynn had fallen to the floor. She was rushed to the hospital by ambulance.

Ella did not know who to call. She had never heard Katlynn talk of family. So, she called Damian. She and Damian went to the hospital with her. After she was admitted and brought up to a room Ella left. Katlynn laid in a bed in the cardiac care unit of the hospital, tubes coming out of her body. She lay unconscious in the dark room; monitors softly beeping occasionally. Only Damian stayed. He was sitting in the chair beside her bed holding her hand when Katlynn opened her eyes.

The room was still dark with a low glow from the hallway. She looked down at her hand, and Damian quickly let go. Softly she asked him where she was and what had happened.

He told her that she had passed out in her office and that she was in the hospital. They were waiting for the test results. She was too weak to talk so she drifted off to sleep.

Damian did not know why he had put her hand into his; it felt good and he took comfort. He knew she was his boss, but he thought of her as a friend as well. And maybe, just maybe, he realized how much he liked Katlynn. She did not talk of family as she was a very private person, but somehow, he knew that she had a heart for family just like his Italian heritage. Maybe they were kindred spirits with both of their pasts a little jolted from the normal. Was there really normal anymore? Maybe family is not always about blood, but who was there to support you. He always felt Katlynn supported him and yes, the other employees, too. But she was there for him when he had a wounded heart. Good friends were hard to find. In a lifetime you only get a few. And when you find them, they bless you. It was scaring him as he thought about holding her hand. What would she say? Would she remember? What was he thinking?

The doctor came into the room and touched her shoulder. She opened her eyes and tried to sit up. "Just lay back and rest, Katlynn. You have had a mild heart attack. Nothing major this time, but we need to find out what caused it and you need rest. "

Katlynn looked over at Damian and stretched out her hand. He took her hand in his again and held it tight. She drifted off to sleep again. He asked Ella to look around in Katlynn's office and find her phone. He would call her mother to come. He wanted to be the one who called.

Maggie could not understand who would be calling her this late at night as she fumbled for the phone on her nightstand, almost knocking it to the floor. She looked at the number and saw that it was Katlynn.

"Hello sweetie. Is everything okay? Do you realize it is after midnight?" Maggie was still trying to focus her eyes in the dark room.

"I am sorry, but this is Damian, not Katlynn. I work for her and I need to tell you something. She is in the hospital in the cardiac care unit."

Maggie sat up and turned the light on. "What? What happened? Is she going to be okay?" She began to cry.

Damian was not good at this, he thought. "Yes, the doctor says she had a mild heart attack, but will stay for a while in the hospital and then she would need to take time off from work."

Maggie began to cry again. "My poor daughter all alone. I should be there. Oh, I do not know what to do." Maggie seemed at a loss for words, her emotions and mind racing in every direction.

Damian said, "I will arrange for you to come. I will call you back with the airline information and will have someone pick you up at the airport."

Maggie asked him why he was not going to pick her up. He said he would not leave Katlynn's side. Maggie hung up and began to put some things into her suitcase. Damian. Who was this Damian? Katlynn had not mentioned that she was seeing anyone. But then again, they had not been one for deep communication in the last few years.

She found herself on a plane heading to New York. She looked out the window at the stars. Maggie had a random thought. "Maybe they are not really stars, but rather openings in heaven where the love of our loved ones pours through."

She felt the jolt of the landing and was ready to get off the plane to see her loved one; her only precious daughter. Ella,

Katlynn's assistant whom she had heard of, picked her up from the airport and took her directly to Katlynn. Katlynn lay so still on the sheets, her breath so shallow that Maggie had to stop to see if she was breathing. Damian stood up to greet her when she finally entered the room. "Tall dark and handsome," thought Maggie. He had the same build as her Jim but with darker hair and detailed features. Italian. That is what he was, she thought.

Maggie kissed her daughter on the head and Katlynn opened her eyes. "Mama." She smiled. "How did you know? How did you get here?"

"Your friend Damian took care of everything."

Damian watched Katlynn's face to see if it was okay. He had not asked her and had not known how she would react. But to Damian family was everything. Even if they were broken, broken pieces could always be put back together. That is what he always thought.

Katlynn took her mama's hand and squeezed it and then went back to sleep. This was the routine for 3 weeks until they released her to go home. Maggie stayed with her for another two weeks; Damian coming over in the evening after work for a while. He said it was to give Maggie a break, but it was to spend time with Katlynn.

Katlynn sat on the couch next to Damian and put her feet in his lap. "I want to get back to work. I am ready."

Damian looked at her and smiled. "You are weaker than you think. You need to rest and get well. Work will be there when you get back."

"But I need to have a purpose; I miss being out in the field. I want to go out in the field again. By the way, have you heard from Matthew? He was supposed to meet with me that day I collapsed."

Damian shifted on the couch and looked at her. "Matthew has just gotten back from California reporting on the mudslides there." Katlynn put her feet on the floor and stood. She walked to the refrigerator and took out a diet soda. She sat across from him. Damian asked, "Katlynn, aren't you originally from North Carolina?"

"Yes, I grew up in Wake Forest, NC, but was born and lived my small childhood in Harkers Island."

Damian took her hand. "Well, there is a category 4 hurricane heading straight to that part of North Carolina. It looks like Harkers Island is going to take a direct hit."

Katlynn began to cry softly and Damian held her in his arms for what seemed a long time to comfort her. Memories, horrible memories flooded her mind.

Chapter 6

For the next few days Damian and Katlynn were glued to the television, the internet and any other media they could consume as they watched satellite images of a Category 4 hurricane reported on September 5, 2018. The eye was massive and it scared both of them. How could anyone survive this? Then on September 7, 2018 it dropped to a Category 2. Yet at a Category 2 the winds were still at 110 miles per hour and could destroy anything in its path.

The next two days Damian came over after work bringing dinner; they watched the television as they ate. On September 9 Florence was downgraded to a Category 1. But still it was a dangerous storm with 74 to 95 mph and gusts of 110 mph winds. Danger would be from falling debris, trees and downed power lines, roofs being ripped off and of course the danger of flooding.

Katlynn snuggled closer to Damian as they continued to watch the news. He noticed this and put his arm around her. She did not push him away. He began to wonder what this all meant. Was he a good friend, comforting her? She was his boss so it felt awkward, yet it felt good. He had always admired Katlynn for her beauty and brains. She was not like any boss he had ever worked for. She allowed her employees to be free spirits and yet she kept close reigns on them for good journalism. She trusted her employees to be creative and he liked that about her. She was not one of those bosses who micromanage everyone; yet she still had a pulse on the work and demanded quality. That was why she was so successful. That was why her team was successful, too. He wondered to himself how and when did this shift change. If he would admit it, he could fall in love with Katlynn. Then he wondered to himself again that he did not know much about her personal life at all. Would she share? She knew a lot about him. She knew about how his parents died, how he was raised by his Italian grandmother, how family was so important to him although he did not have much family connections now that his grandparents had died.

Katlynn shifted again on the couch; her head heavy. He realized she had fallen asleep. He laid her down on the couch and covered her with the throw. He turned the television off, left the lamp on and wrote her a quick note. He shut the door softly as to not awaken her and left.

Driving home, he began to panic. When she got fully well and did not need his assistance then what? Would she look at him differently? How would it affect their working relationship? Could he just pretend that it never happened? Nothing had really happened and yet she put her feet in his lap and he had rubbed them, he had held her when she was crying and scared, she had snuggled against him and scooted closer to him tonight. Should he make an excuse tomorrow after work and not show up? Should he bring some of the other coworkers with him? He was so confused and thinking about her that he almost forgot his turn off the highway. He made a quick turn onto the ramp. When he got home, he would try to sleep and deal with this in the morning.

Daylight shown through the blinds and shone on Katlynn's face awakening her. She sat up, squinted in the morning light, trying to figure out where she was. When she realized she had fallen asleep on the couch she jolted up and checked her front door. It was locked. As she turned to turn the lamp off, she saw the note.

Katlynn, you fell asleep and looked so tired that I laid you down and covered you. I hope you have a good night's sleep. You still need the rest to heal.

Signed,

Damian

Katlynn looked at the note. She reread it. It said nothing about him coming over tonight. Nor did he say what time he left. He just signed the note SIGNED Damian. SIGNED. What was she expecting, she thought? It was not like they were together. What were they? She was his boss, that was for sure, but he had been there for her when she collapsed. And his was the first face she saw when she woke up in the intensive care unit. He was holding her hand. Did that mean anything? Or was he just a good employee and a good friend? And yet he was the one who had been with her every night after work since her mama went back home. She got into the shower and dressed to go out. She had not been outside since her hospital stay. Maybe today she would go for a slow walk at the park to get some fresh air. She would take her phone in case she needed it.

The park was empty today; unlike the weekend when she came to run track. The breeze softly swayed the trees as if they were dancing on this beautiful September day. She remembered another September day long ago. The one where the threat of a storm was imminent, the one where her daddy drove her to what would be a new life, where that would be the last time that she would see him. Did he know that it would be the last time? Sometimes she thought back and thought maybe he didn't. He and his family had been through hurricanes before and survived. If he had known it would be the last time would he have hugged her and mama a little longer?

She was tired. More tired than she thought she would be. She made it back to the house. It was noon and the phone rang. Damian. But it was not Damian. It was Maggie. "Hi. I wanted to check on you today. How is it going?"

"I just got back from a slow walk and it felt like I had run a marathon. The doctor is right. I do need to rest, but I get so bored and then I think I am feeling much better than I am." Katlynn filled up a water bottle from the sink.

"Do you want me to come to help you again? I can cancel my classes and come if you need me to."

"No, I am doing okay. My friends are checking on me quite regularly." Although it was late afternoon and she had not heard from Damian.

"Well, okay, if you need me to come back just let me know. I will talk to you later. I love you Sweet Pea. Goodbye." Maggie hung up.

Sweet Pea. She had not been called that in a long, long time. That is what her daddy used to call her. Katlynn was tempted to call Damian, but did not want to seem so needy. She would call Ella instead.

"Ella, it is Katlynn. I thought I would call and see how things are going without me."

Ella laughed, "It is bumping along okay, but you are sure missed. Mr. Gordon is keeping his thumb on everyone and is heavily involved in everything they are doing. He is even assigning them all jobs to do. You know how well that is going over," Ella laughing again.

"I can only imagine. I go back to the doctor in two weeks. Surely, he will allow me to come back, even if it is for only half a day," Katlynn said hopefully.

"Lindsay and Cameron have been sent out together to Washington, DC to cover some political story. Mr. Gordon of course got push back because those two are so different from each other and hate politics. He said he did not care; he was paying them and to go and produce," Ella volunteered all the details to Katlynn.

Katlynn waited to see if she would volunteer information on Damian and Matt, but she did not. So, she carefully asked. "What does he have Damian and Matt assigned to?" She let out a breath, not realizing she had been holding it.

Ella was quiet for a moment and replied, "I do not know. Mr. Gordon told me it was a secret assignment and they would report to him directly."

Katlynn held her breath again. "What kind of secret assignment? He is not sending them into a war zone I hope!"

Ella did not know what to say. She had not thought of that, but it was odd that he was keeping it from her as she always knew where everyone was and what their itinerary was.

"Keep me posted if you find out anything." Katlynn hung up and noticed that it was dark already outside. No Damian. No dinner. No phone calls. She wasn't hungry anyway; she went to bed.

Maggie was just stepping out of the shower when the phone rang; she picked it up on the 4th ring. It was Damian. Of course, she was concerned that something else had happened to Katlynn. She sat down on the edge of the bed in case it was bad news.

Damian began, "I am sorry to bother you this late, Maggie, but Matt and I are headed to North Carolina to cover a story. We have to stay in the Raleigh area for a few days when we arrive. We both have hotel rooms, but I thought if you did not mind, I could come by to see you."

"Is everything okay with Katlynn? Are you coming by to see me with bad news? Just tell me now, Damian." Maggie began to wring her hands in nervousness.

"No, it is not that at all. We are coming to cover Hurricane Florence. Katlynn does not know about this. Mr. Gordon has assigned this to us and has asked us to keep it from her. I did not tell her that I was leaving. I just found out last night after I left her place myself. So please do not let her know I am going to be in North Carolina for a while." Damian did not like deceit, but he also needed his job and for some reason Mr. Gordon had asked him to be confidential this time.

Damian and Matt arrived in Raleigh, North Carolina on September 11, 2018. And on September 13, 2018 Hurricane Florence made landfall. It would be two weeks before they could leave Raleigh area and drive the rental car to the coast. They learned that all of the Eastern North Carolina Coastal communities, especially around Harkers Island, had been ordered to evacuate. But they found out that a lot of people did not leave. The storm came ashore with 90 mph winds and terrifying storm surges, splintering buildings and trapping people in high water as it settled for what could be a long and destructive drenching. It was also a 400-mile-wide hurricane that pounded away and unloaded 36 inches of rain and it flattened trees and knocked out power for over 600,000 homes and businesses. Crops were damaged, 1.7 million chickens were killed and 42 people died in this storm.

To add to the injury 16 rivers crested adding to the destruction. More than 12,000 people were in the shelters; homes and apartments were so damaged most folks had to move away inland or to stay in the shelters long term while waiting for FEMA, the National Guard, American Red Cross, Salvation Army, churches, non-profits and citizens come to the rescue.

When Matt and Damian arrived to Harkers Island they had to stay in the shelter, too. Hotels were damaged as well. Matt loved this type of reporting. He loved facts, data and timelines. He loved to take photos and be out in the field with his gear and laptop. Damian, however, stayed behind. He lived with the people in the shelter, going out some to see their homes and the destruction. One day he decided to go up to a house and knock on the door. On the mailbox was the name Harcourt. He wondered if they were kin to Katlynn.

He had spent some time with Maggie who confided in him the very personal aspects of Katlynn's childhood. She would be upset if she knew he and her mama had talked. Maggie was very open to him; she trusted him and seemed to like him. He liked her, too. He missed having a mama and family connections.

He walked up the sidewalk to a small home. The outside of the house looked like it had not seen paint in years. The boards on the porch were loose; the screen door torn. It was not from the storm, but from years of neglect. He saw that some of the roof was missing and a tree had fallen on the shed in the backyard. He knocked softly at first. No one came to the door. He knocked louder, yet no one came. They probably had evacuated, he thought. When he turned to walk down the steps a man was there at the sidewalk. Damian introduced himself and they went inside the house to talk.

Chapter 7

Katlynn held her cup of hot tea as she watched CNN news tell of Hurricane Florence slamming the coast of North Carolina. She took a sip and set it down on the coffee table as she pulled the throw up to her neck. It was not cold inside the house, but she felt cold. She watched the predictions and watched as the news crews tried to get close. It was too dangerous with the waters covering Highway 70 and also I40 in Wilmington, NC for the news crews to get close just yet. She bent over and picked up the TV remote and pushed the power off button. She could not watch it anymore. She decided to call her mama.

Maggie had been watching the news as well and had just turned it off as the phone rang. It startled her. "Hello." Maggie sounded out of breath, but she was just anxious.

"Mama, are you okay? You sound out of breath," Katlynn asked.

"No, I have been glued to the TV for the past three hours. I just got tired of all the talking. The news crews will not know anything for a few days," Maggie sighed.

There was silence for a moment and then Katlynn began. "Mama, I cannot remember much about that night we left. I have tried, but I guess the years have made it all fade. I can only remember sitting in the car in the backseat with my stuffed animals and clothes. It was late and I was sleepy. I do remember that. Daddy picked you up from the diner. You got in the car with your apron still on. You seemed angry that daddy did not want to go back by the house; he just drove what seemed like all night."

Katlynn continued. "Then I remember getting there and he carrying me up to my new room to bed. He kissed me on my cheek and called me Sweet Pea and then put a picture of me and him in my hand. And then he was gone."

Maggie breathed deep before she talked. "Yes, that was pretty much it."

"Mama, I am a grown woman now. Please tell me why we had to leave and why he stayed. Why would he not want to come with us?" Maggie thought she heard Katlynn sniffle.

"It is complicated. I begged him to come with us. Somehow, I just knew the storm would destroy everything. Little did I know then how it would destroy *everything*, including my family. Oh, how I loved your daddy, but like your grandma always said, "He has salt water in his blood." I did not understand that at the time, but now I know. The people of Harkers Island are bonded together like a deep thread that connects family and friends alike. When I found out his brother and your cousin were evacuating, I could not get inside his head to make him leave too."

Maggie paused and wet her lips. "I do have regrets, Katlynn. I wanted a life here for the both of us in Wake Forest, NC. We were on our way to our dream life and Jim seemed happy. But family ties called and he went to them. I went with him, but I never fit in because I was selfish and was sad and did not want to live there. I wish I had embraced our time together. If you find someone who adores you and you fall in love, go where he wants to go. That is my advice."

Katlynn thought about that a moment. "Mama that still does not answer my question as to why he left us."

Maggie could hear the sniffles again.

"Oh, honey, I have asked myself that question over and over again and still have no answer. I have beat myself up and replayed it over in my mind and still it comes out the same. So, I just moved on and thank God for the time that we **did have** and for him giving me you." Now Maggie was sniffling.

"Mama, how do you know when you are in love? How do you tell?"

Maggie smiled and wiped her eyes. "Oh, honey, you will know it deep inside. When he is gone from you there is a burning longing and loss. You cannot wait to hear his voice or see him again. Is there someone you would like to tell me about?"

"No. I mean I do not know. I guess being alone without you and Aunt Sophia and other family being sick and, in the hospital, has got me to thinking and missing family. It is also like I am missing something." Katlynn really wanted to tell her mama that she thought she loved Damian, but if he had loved her back, he would have called. It had been a couple of weeks now. She wondered what she had done for him to not call.

Maggie asked about her employees and if she had heard from any of them. Katlynn told of how her boss had taken over and how she heard through the grapevine how they hated it and missed her direction. They talked a while and then Katlynn told her about Damian.

"Mama, I do not know what to do. Damian is my employee, and a good friend, and he has been at my side through all of my illness and yet he just disappeared. Of course, Ella says he is on an assignment that she doesn't even know about. That concerns me. But you think he would have called by now." Katlynn waited for a reply.

Maggie, knowing where Damian was, tried to not lie to her daughter, but tried to keep the confidence Damian had requested. She squirmed a little before she began. "I thought you gave assignments and did not micro manage them."

Katlynn replied, "I do, but that is not how it usually works."

Maggie said, "But you are not even supposed to be at work so they are probably just trying to let you rest. You will get back to knowing details when you officially return to work. Just try to enjoy your time off and not worry so."

Katlynn thought about that; it made sense. Then she thought about just texting Damian to see if he would answer. She told Maggie her plan and hung up. Maggie said a little prayer. She did not want her to get hurt.

She paced back and forth in the living room. Should she text him? What if he ignored her? What if he was somewhere where he could not answer her? How would she know the difference? She made all kinds of excuses as she held her phone and wore out a piece of the carpet pacing like a caged animal. Being a journalist and writer, she began asking herself why she wanted to contact him. She could not answer that question. She called her best friend and talked to her about it. Her friend told her to just contact him. Subconsciously she must like him a lot and not admitting it. She hung up.

Katlynn took a shower, got into the bed and turned the lamp on to read. She read two chapters and laid the book back down. She picked up her phone and put in Damian's phone number. She texted him a message. "Hi. Just thinking about you tonight. Hope all is well. Text me. Katlynn."

She pushed *send*. She watched her phone until she saw the word *sent*. Then she laid down across her bed and went soundly to sleep. She woke in the morning to find her phone somewhere lost in the covers. When she found it there was no return message, she began to cry. She was angry with herself as she had become so emotional since she collapsed. She had never acted like this before. The phone rang and it startled her. Maggie was on the other end. She could tell she was crying.

"Katlynn, I will come there again if you need me. Or I can come and get you and bring you here. What is it, baby?"

"Mama, I texted Damian and he did not answer me. I feel like such a fool. I am so emotional and out of control since I got sick. He is a good friend. But I thought there might be something growing between us; something good. How wrong I was and now I feel like a fool." Katlynn was crying hard now.

Maggie had never in her life broke a confidence of someone, but she felt she should this time. It bothered her to even try. "Katlynn, I have never in my life, and I mean never never, broken a confidence when someone confided in me. God forgive me for this."

Katlynn was curious and wondered what in the world her mama was talking about. "Mama, what is it?"

"Damian came to see me. He is in North Carolina. He will be here for a while on assignment and asked me to not worry you. Now I feel so bad. But I am not going to tell you where or what, so hopefully it will not be too big a sin. Although sin in any form is bad."

"Mama, you take religion too seriously," Katlynn replied.

This angered Maggie. "No, Katlynn, I do not! God is the most important and He tells us how to live and how to treat others. The bible is a whole book of instructions on living. If anything I do regret, it is that I did not make you go with me and Sophia to church. You were too young to make that decision and I was in such grief that I did not make good decisions for you. I am sorry, dear. I must hang up now."

Maggie hung up. Katlynn looked at her phone and shook her head. She went outside to her patio that overlooked the street of New York City. People and cars were scurrying around like ants. Is this what God sees when he looks down from heaven? People busy going and coming; people too busy to stop and even nod a head or wave at someone on the sidewalk? She could not remember a lot about her childhood, but she could remember sitting in that small white wooden church as she sat between her mama and daddy. She could remember the preacher telling her that God was up there in heaven looking down and yet he did not just see the whole world full of people- he could see her as a small child; each individually. He would not force himself on anyone, but anyone who needed him could call on him and he would be there to help. She remembered one day she could not find Rascal. He had been missing for two days. She went out to the dock and got on her knees and asked God to find her dog. He answered her prayer as the next morning she heard barking at the front door.

She could not remember when the last time was when she had asked God for something. Or when she had asked God for help in decisions she needed to make. Or when she had asked him for discernment on things she needed. Katlynn was a list maker. So, she got out a pad and pen and began to write her list. She needed help with this health issue. She needed help to know if she was really falling in love with Damian or if he was just a need that needed filling. She needed help with making decisions on her life; this illness had begun to put life into perspective. She needed help in moving forward; but especially in forgiving. She needed help in forgiving her mama, her daddy and her own self. She needed help in forgiving God who took her dreams and life as she knew it away. But how does one even begin? She had not been in church in so long. Did she need to go to church to begin? She Googled it and came up with websites that were not much help. So, she crawled into bed - it was only 8:30pm- and ran everything through her mind. All she could say was 'Jesus' as she pulled the covers over her head and tried to go to sleep.

Her phone dinged twice and lit up the room. It was a text from Damian. It said, "If this is a good time call me."

Her heart raced. Her mind raced. What was she going to say to him? She thought about ignoring it like he had ignored her days before. But he may had been in a zone with no coverage. She reached for her glass of water beside the bed and took a sip. Then she punched his number. It rang.

"Hello." Damian sounded good yet frustrated.

"Hi, it is Katlynn. It is good to hear your voice. I have missed you." She hoped that did not sound too bad.

"I have missed you too. Maggie called me upset. I am sorry that I put her in such a predicament. She is a good Godly woman, Katlynn, and it has hurt me that I have hurt her. I hope she can forgive me. She says that she has. We both have the same goal. To help her daughter." Damian's voice was softer than she remembered.

"Damian, I feel so bad. Messing up people's lives in what I apparently do best. Good people come my way and then I push them far away. I am not proud of that. I do not know how to change that. If you do not mind me asking, where are you?"

"I have been in Beaufort and now am in Harkers Island after the hurricane. Matt and I are covering a story of the flooding and devastation. Of course, I am supposed to keep this from you, but I do not like keeping things from the people I love." Damian waited for her reaction.

"Damian, do you mean love like a good friend? Or do you mean love like love?" Katlynn felt herself blush but she needed to know.

"Katlynn, what do you want it to be? You tell me and then I will tell you."

"Okay. I am putting my heart and trust out on the table. Damian, I love you. Not just friend or employee love, but love you deeply. I have realized how much I have missed you and how much I really love you. There. I said it." Katlynn waited for his response.

"Katlynn, I love you, too. But when I get back to New York we need to talk. It will be another week before I get back. Before we go further into this relationship, we need to both be on the same page. Call your mama. I will be back in 7 days and will talk to you then. I love you." Damian hung up.

Katlynn began to shake. And she began to pray. A real prayer with words this time. Then she called her mama.

Chapter 8

It was time for Katlynn to go back to work. She had been wishing for this day for six weeks; and yet it was here and she was not ready. She had done a lot of thinking these past weeks. Soul searching as her mama would say. Katlynn looked in her closet for something to wear. Everything looked tired to her. She found a blue jean skirt and a pink blouse. She put on some pink ice earrings and a little blush on her face. The pink made her look healthy and happy. Oh, she was pretty healthy after all she had been through. She was still sorting out happy.

She rode the elevator up to her floor and got off. Looking in her purse she found her office key and went in. She flipped the light on and there were her coworkers. A large banner was taped to her desk. WELCOME BACK! On the side table were snacks; healthy kinds of foods. On a chair were gifts. They all yelled welcome back when she came into the room. There were hugs and high fives and clapping. After she got over the initial shock she began to laugh. "Okay, are you trying to give me another heart attack?" she asked playfully. They all laughed and smiled. They ate and she opened the gifts from each one. There were stress balls, sea breeze smelling body lotion, a scented candle of jasmine, a leather notebook and pen and some dark chocolate with a note that said research says dark chocolate is good for your heart. Soon everyone went back to their desks to work and she was alone with Damian. She was looking over her gifts and realized that she received a gift from everyone but him.

Damian was sitting behind her desk in her chair. Katlynn began, "You look too comfortable there. Do you want my job?" She sat down in the chair across from him.

"No, Katlynn, I do not want your job. As a matter of fact, I may not want my job. I have been doing a lot of reflecting and serious thinking these past weeks." He swirled the chair around and looked out at the New York skyline.

"Look at these tall buildings. Nothing but concrete and people. People everywhere. Do you hear that, Katlynn?" He waited for her to answer.

"No, what is it I am supposed to hear?" She looked confused.

"So, you're telling me you do not hear anything?" Damian turned away from the window and looked Katlynn in the eyes.

"No, Damian. I do not." She was getting frustrated.

"Close your eyes. I will tell you what you should be hearing."

Katlynn closed her eyes and Damian began. "Listen to all the sounds of the cars and large trucks. Do you hear the taxis beeping their horn as they weave in and out of traffic as they try to get one car length ahead? Do you hear sirens? Police cars, ambulances going to some tragedy. People yelling to each other in the streets; even if it does seem like a friendly yell."

"May I open them now?" Katlynn asked.

"No. Do you hear the sounds of the copier printing page after page outside your door? Do you hear the buzz of the lights above? Now I am finished. Open your eyes." Damian watched as she slowly opened them.

"I guess I have been in the city too long. It is normal; I do not even hear or think about it anymore."

"Exactly," Damian said. "Exactly. We go at such a fast pace that we do not hear anymore, Katlynn. We do not hear between the lines, even."

"What do you mean?"

"That we are so busy doing that we do not even realize when we have fallen in love with someone. We are too busy to take the time or make the time for relationships. We spend all day holding these phones, iPads and listening for the ding of a computer to tell us that we have an email or a Facebook post." Damian took his hand and brushed it through his hair.

He stood up and came over to Katlynn and took her hands into his. He kissed her softly, a gentle kiss and stepped back.

"We are too busy that we do not see either Katlynn." Damian walked around the room and waved his hands.

"Do you see anymore, Katlynn?" Damian came back over to her and pulled her out of the chair. She stood and he embraced her with a long hug. Then he took her hand and led her to her chair behind the desk- the desk that said Editor in Chief. She sat down and he said he would let her get to work. He said they would go out to dinner tonight. He wanted to see her away from the office. If she could get away from the office at least by 7pm he would meet her at the Italian Restaurant down the street a block. Then he blew her a kiss and shut her door.

Katlynn wondered what in the world had happened to him. He was gone a couple of weeks and something had changed him. She closed her eyes again to listen to the city. She could hear all those things if she sat quietly and intentionally. She opened her eyes and looked around the room. What had Damian meant by 'seeing'? Katlynn booted her computer up and began to go through all the emails. She sorted them by what she deemed important and which ones she needed to reply to promptly. She made folders and made notes for new assignments that she wanted her team to accomplish. She worked all day, almost skipping lunch. She would have skipped it like so many times before if not for Ella. Ella brought them both salads and came into the office. They both even had a bite of the dark chocolate for dessert. Ella walked to the door to leave. As she had her hand on the door to close it, she said, "Katlynn, I just love your new picture." Then she shut the door.

Katlynn looked puzzled. What was Ella talking about? Damian had just accused her of not hearing and seeing. And now this? He had not even given her a present. Maybe he was going to give her something special when she saw him for dinner tonight. She picked up the plates from the Deli they had just ate and put them in the trash can. She looked up at the wall and then was when she saw it. There hanging on the wall with all the "important" art was a 16 x 20 photo that was framed. It was of her and her daddy on the shrimping boat. She ran over to the picture and starred. Then she found her purse and opened her wallet. There was the original photo as it had always been, safe in her wallet. Her heart began to race. How did it get there? Who had this done? Was it Damian? It must have been him. He told her earlier that she could not hear nor see anymore. But when, why and how? She was beginning to get angry. Had he gone into her purse when she was sick? How did he get it? Why would he do such a thing? Could she trust him? It made no sense. So, she called her mama.

"Mama, I want you to be honest with me right now," Katlynn asked when Maggie had just said the word Hello.

"Katlynn, is that you?" Maggie did not recognize her own daughter's voice.

"I am sorry, mama, it is just that I came back to work today and it is stressful. And hanging in my office is a picture of me and daddy. The one he handed me when he left." Katlynn's hands were sweaty.

"Do you have a photo like mine? Did you give it to Damian?" Katlynn asked accusingly.

"Slow down. No, I do not have that photo. And no, I did not get it from Damian. Have you asked him if he was the one who had it done?" Maggie asked point blank.

"No. It is just I do not know how it could have been done without someone going through my purse and taking something out of my wallet. I do not like that, mama. So, if you or Damian did it while I was sick and, in the hospital, and out of it, I want to know." Katlynn had an accusing tone to her voice.

"No, we did not go through your things. How dare you think that either one of us would do that. I am surprised and disappointed that you would even think such a thing. I am late for an appointment so I must go." Maggie hung up.

Katlynn looked at time on her phone. It was already 7:30pm. She was late for dinner. She shut her computer down and turned off the office lights. Everyone else had already left for the day. The whole office had a warm glow from lamps on the desks as the overhead lights were off. She locked her door and pushed the elevator button. When she reached the restaurant, the waitress told her Damian had left.

She ordered something to go and went home. She was tired after a 14-hour day. She ate and laid down on the couch. Soon she was fast asleep. She opened her eyes. It was 1:30am.

She reached for her phone and texted Damian. "Hello. I am sorry I missed you for dinner."

She waited. She waited some more. Finally, he answered. "Fourteen hours a day again. Really Katlynn? Did you not learn anything from this illness?" He pushed 'send.'

"Apparently not. Lol. But seriously, Damian, I did 'see' something today. It was a framed photo of me and daddy." Katlynn pushed 'send.'

"Good. I will see you tomorrow. We can try this again tomorrow night. See if you can be on time."

"Do you know how it got there? Where did the photo come from?" Katlynn pushed 'send' and wished she could retrieve. It sounded accusatory.

"Oh my. How untrusting and making assumptions. Not only can you not hear or see but now you are making assumptions." Damian pushed 'send' and waited for her reply.

"I think this conversation is over. Apparently, I do not know you very well Damian. I thought I did, but apparently I was wrong." Katlynn punched the send button hard.

"I want to talk to you face to face. We will do this at a reasonable hour, Katlynn. Go to bed and get rest before you go back into the hospital. Goodnight." Damian pushed 'send' and turned off his phone.

Katlynn was somewhere between curious, angry and hurt. She could not put a finger on which one it truly was. She pulled the photo out of her wallet and laid it beside her bed. She fell back to sleep. Sunlight drifted between the blinds and woke her. She had overslept. She rushed to find clothes and to hurry to the office. She drove through Starbucks for a large coffee.

She then realized that she was doing the same pattern that she had before her collapse. Not good, she thought. She would find Damian first thing this morning and they would go out to breakfast. She was his boss, so he would have to go.

As soon as the elevator door opened, he was standing there. He looked like he had not slept. He took her arm and gently led her back into the elevator. He pushed the down button. She did not argue. They went out onto the sidewalk. He held her hand and led her to the park. He sat down on the park bench and looked up at her.

"I did not sleep. I have not eaten. I went through the drive through and got a large Starbucks coffee in which I tossed. Can we get something for breakfast?" Katlynn watched as he stood up and took her in his arms.

"Let's go back to your place. It is closer than mine. I will cook you breakfast. We must talk." They walked hand in hand back to her apartment.

Chapter 9

Katlynn took her key and unlocked the door. She was headed toward the kitchen. Damian stopped her. "I want you to sit. I will cook you breakfast. I want you to relax and be still. Can you do that for me, Katlynn?"

"Yes, I will try. That is all that I have been doing for the past six weeks." Katlynn took off her shoes and sat on the couch. She picked up a magazine and began to read. Then she put it down. She began to think about what Damian had said about her; the part of not hearing or seeing anymore. She was a journalist and a great one at that. She had all the accolades and trophies to prove it. A good journalist is all about the facts. A good journalist is always looking for the answers to who, what, when, where and how. She had always thought of herself as professional and on top of it all. But her mind kept going back to what Damian had said.

She closed her eyes. She listened to what was in the background. She could hear Damian clanging pots and dishes. She could hear bacon sizzling in the pan. She could hear him whistling as he worked. She could smell the food cooking. It made her smile. She opened her eyes. Then she shut them again. What did she see? Could you 'see' with your eyes closed?

Then she saw in her mind a black dog named Rascal running toward her so fast that he knocked her down. She could see him licking her face as she tried to turn over and get up. She could see her mama on the back porch calling her to come and eat. She could see her daddy coming into the back door of the kitchen, smacking her mama on her bottom as he walked to the sink to wash his hands. She could see the table laden with shrimp from the days catch along with fresh vegetables from the garden. She could see the sun set from the dock in their backyard as it splashed colors of yellow, pink and blue across the sky. She could see the full moon in the dark black sky as stars seemed to wink at her in their twinkle.

She opened her eyes. Then she closed them again. She could see the back seat of a car laden with blankets and pillows as her daddy drove through the night. She could hear the silence between her parents. She could see her daddy putting that photo in her hand and closing her hand around it. She could see his back as he walked away. She opened her eyes again.

Damian came through the kitchen door wearing her pink lacy apron. This made her laugh. She laughed a deep belly laugh. She had not laughed so hard in a long time.

"You think something is funny?" Damian came over to her and took her by the hand. "Breakfast is served, my dear."

Katlynn took a seat and said, "Can you please take that off? Pink is not your color."

Damian playfully said, "Then you need to buy me a manly apron if you want me to cook for you again."

They held hands and said the blessing. He had cooked bacon, made French toast with a bourbon maple syrup with blueberries.

"This is the most delicious meal I have ever eaten," Katlynn said with her mouth full.

"Then you have not lived until you try my Italian grandmother's recipes," Damian replied.

After they ate, they both worked to clean up the kitchen. It felt good to do this together. Katlynn had never had a man cook for her before. She liked it.

They sat on her porch overlooking the city. She pulled her chair close to his.

"The city is noisy today. I have been thinking about what you said about me not hearing. You are right. And also, about me not seeing; although I am still a little confused about that." Katlynn waited for his reply.

He said nothing. So, she waited and then she spoke. "I did see something in my office. Of course, it was mid-day before I noticed it. It was a new picture added to my wall."

He still said nothing. She waited again. He finally spoke. "What was your reaction? Sorry I missed it."

She did not want to say. Damian kept pushing her to tell him. She said, "If you must know the truth, I was angry and confused. I wanted to know..."

Before she could answer he said, "who, what, when, where and how. You wanted the facts instead of enjoying the photo.

You made assumptions and took off from there." Damian watched her face to see her reaction.

"Did you talk to Maggie?" Katlynn said accusatory again.

"No, I did not. But I know you, Katlynn. You are all about the facts and yet deep somewhere in there, as he poked her shirt near her heart, is a totally different person. One who had been lost for a long time."

Katlynn got up and went inside. Damian did not follow. She came back with her wallet in her hand. She opened it and took out the photo of her and her daddy; the one now hanging on her office wall.

Damian stood up. He reached in his back pocket and took out his wallet. In his wallet was the same photo. He handed it to her.

With a shaky voice Katlynn asked, "How did you get this? Where did you get this?"

Damian took another photo out of his wallet. It was one of a young brown-haired girl with a black dog. They were laying in the yard, looking up at the clouds.

Katlynn was visibly shaking now. "Damian, please tell me. Where did you get these?"

96

He led her back into the house and held her in his arms. "Katlynn Harcourt, do you want me to be the reporter and tell you my story for the article that Matt and I were on assignment? Or do you want to *hear* the real story and not just the facts.

Katlynn looked into his eyes. They were teary eyed. She had never seen Damian like that before. "Damian, I want to hear from your heart. No reporting, no facts. Please, I promise I will hear and see with my heart."

So, Damian began. He began with the trip to North Carolina. He included seeing Maggie and talking to her before the trip to Harkers Island. He spoke of the devastation, flooding, ripped up roofs and trees everywhere that Hurricane Florence left in her path.

He spoke of seeing dead fish, even in the streets, and the smells of really bad odors. He told her about going to a house that was flooded; the owners were living in a tent in the side yard as they hauled trees and debris toward the street. He told her of FEMA, church groups, the Salvation Army and the American Red Cross there with food to feed the hungry. He began to cry when he told her of the people from the churches coming to help with supplies and labor to help those in more need than they had.

Then he told her of a man on a shrimping boat trying to fix the nets and picking up parts that were floating in the water nearby. The man was struggling and looked in need of help. So, Damian said he took off his shoes, rolled up his pant legs and waded into the water to help the man. He helped him retrieve what they could get. Then he helped him sweep out mud and water from his house. It had flooded the front two rooms of his house.

He learned the man's name was Bobby. Bobby Harcourt cooked this stranger from the big city of New York some shrimp and grits for dinner. It was the last of all he had. Damian said he shared some drinks and snacks from his cooler he had brought along in his truck. They sat by the fire and listened to the water lap; saw the stars and moon come out.

Damian had been there all day. He was sure Matt was looking for him, but the cell phone coverage was not working due to the storm. And anyway, he had let the cell phone die. Damian told Katlynn it had been a long time since he had seen or heard, too.

Katlynn was crying now. Just softly as she continued to listen. She wanted to ask questions, but decided to just hear and see for a change.

Damian told her at the end of the day he asked Bobby Harcourt if he knew Katlynn. He asked if she had sent him on an assignment. He told him honestly that she had not. He told Bobby that he had just happened to stop here today, by chance. Bobby told him nothing was by chance. That he had been praying for years for that little girl. Bobby took out two photos and put it in his hand. He told Damian that they belonged to him now. To do what he wanted with them. Then he shook Bobby's hand and went to find Matt at the hotel.

Katlynn's face had tears streaming down, but she said nothing.

"I saw that empty spot on your wall. It took me a little while to decide which photo I wanted to have blown up. I chose the one with you and your dad. Bobby Harcourt has some of the same features of your dad." Damian wiped a tear from his face.

Katlynn fell into his arms and sobbed. "Damian, I wanted that photo blown up a long time ago. I was afraid if it went from my possession that it could be lost. If it was lost, then it would gone forever."

Damian held her tight. He replied, "Even if you lost it you would still have the memories. The memories of the laughs, jokes, smiles, conversations, plans, tears and experiences. So long as memories of loved ones lives in your heart you can say that life is good Possession- life is not a possession to be defended, but a gift to be shared."

Katlynn pushed back to see his face. "Thank you for the photo. What else can you tell me?"

Damian replied, "That is enough for this day. We need to go back to work. I think we should keep our relationship professional right now at work until we figure out what we are."

"I agree. I love you, Damian. More than you will ever know."

Chapter 10

Katlynn watched as the snow splattered her office window. She saw a big boom truck with a lift rising with two men. They were putting up a banner that said MACY'S THANKSGIVING PARADE AT 10:30 AM. Thanksgiving. Wow, it had come so soon again. She looked at the calendar. Thanksgiving was in five days. She had always worked the holidays so that her employees could be with their families. And she enjoyed watching the parade from the warmth. For the past several years she had brought a tray of goodies and went down to the fifth floor where she shared food and friendship and watched the parade with others who worked that day, too.

Damian walked into her office just as her cell phone rang. She waved him to come and sit down. It was Maggie. He listened as Katlynn talked to her mama. Maggie asked about the weather and then she asked what she was doing for Thanksgiving this year. Maggie was hoping since Katlynn's illness that she would spend some time with her. Katlynn told her she did not have plans; probably would work and hung up.

Damian furled his brow and looked at her. "Nothing, huh? I thought you were going with me to the Farm to Table in New Hampshire this year." He waited for her response.

"I thought you were just joking. You always in the past worked on some exotic assignment and spent Thanksgiving with whoever. And you always took your best friend Tim."

"Tim got married two months ago," Damian replied. "The owners of Farm to Table contacted me. Since my brilliant article their business is booming. They have had to hire more drivers for their DoorStop Delivery part of their business."

"What is the DoorStop Delivery?" Katlynn asked.

Damian replied, "When customers sign up for Doorstop Delivery, they're assigned a delivery day based on their location. The company runs lean and tries not to do a lot of backtracking on their deliveries. Once they're signed up, customers make their selections and tell them how often they would like their products delivered. Some customers have standing orders: They might order milk, bread, eggs, bacon and a basket of fresh vegetables each week, for example. Their customers could buy it at their local grocery but they know where the food comes from and it is fresh; it has not been on a truck coming across country for weeks to get to the stores."

Katlynn smiled. "It was kind of like my daddy did in Harkers Island. They went out each day shrimping during the season. They sold to restaurants and some out of the back of their pickup trucks to locals."

"Exactly. And since they have done so well financially since my article, they asked me if I wanted anything. No, they cannot deliver to New York from New Hampshire, but she did offer me another ticket to their Thanksgiving Dinner. They were able to expand to five more people." Damian watched Katlynn's face.

"Oh, three tickets?" Katlynn was curious now.

"Yes. I would love for you and Maggie to be my guests."

"You want to invite my mama? How is she going to get there? She does not do well in big cities."

"I plan to fly her here to New York. Then we can get there together from here. I will pay for everything and make the arrangements." Damian leaned back in the chair and stretched his back.

"Why would you want to do that?" It sounded so mean or crass as those words left her mouth.

"Oh, I don't know Katlynn. Maybe because I love you and I love family. I thought it would be a good gesture. Forget it. I thought you would be excited as I am." Damian got up to leave.

"No, don't leave. It is a great idea! I have just been alone for so long it is foreign to me. Let's call her now." Katlynn dialed Maggie's number and put her on speaker phone. Damian told her all about it and how it would work. She was so excited she cried tears of joy.

They arrived to the airport and the DoorStop Delivery van pulled up to pick them up. The driver laughed and was friendly. He said he was used to delivering instead of picking up. They all thought it was funny. Once they got out of the city he drove through the most beautiful countryside. Maggie was in awe of the beauty and did not say a word the whole trip there.

Katlynn gasped as the driver rode them up a two-mile road. At the entrance to the road was the most beautiful streetlamp with lights and horses. Trees lined both sides of the road as they made their way to the barn restaurant. Before they arrived to the barn it began to snow.

The owners were expecting them early. They invited them into their private house for hot chocolate and cookies. They told them of the history of Farm to Table, how it had grown from a small family farm and expanded to a large business. They told them how they came up with the idea for a Thanksgiving dinner for those whose families were far away or just displaced for whatever reason. Damian interjected as to the importance of family, especially to Italian families and their culture. The owners agreed.

They all walked out to the big red barn that looked like a horse stable from the outside. But inside was very beautiful. A long table was set beautifully with Indian corn, apples, squash

105

and greenery. The napkins had a burlap look, although they were soft. There were name plates at each place so their guest would know where to sit. Beside each placemat was a pen and piece of paper. After all was seated, they were asked to write something they were thankful for. Each person put their paper into an empty mason jar. They would be read later.

The food was set up buffet style. The table was laden with fried sage leaves, Tortellini with Zucca, roast lamb, baked holiday squash, rosemary potatoes and chocolate chestnut cake for dessert. There were all kinds of wines, coffee and spiced teas. The guests were from all over the United States; some were Italian, but most were not. Guests just enjoyed their day; no one talked of why they were not with their family that day. The owners requested that people enjoy the new experience and be thankful for 'different' as life changes and we must move like the tide with it. Katlynn thought about that analogy. Then she somehow remembered something her daddy told her about Henry Wadsworth Longfellow. She had forgotten it until they referenced how we must move with the tide. Her daddy had shown her a book in which Henry Wadsworth Longfellow wrote *"The Tide Rises, the Tide Falls"* in 1879 at his summer home on the sea at Nahant, Massachusetts.

The tide rises, the tide falls,

The twilight darkens, the curlew calls;

Along the sea-sands damp and brown

The traveler hastens toward the town,

And the tide rises, the tide falls.

Darkness settles on roofs and walls,

But the sea, the sea in darkness calls;

The little waves, with their soft, white hands

Efface the footprints in the sands,

And the tide rises, the tide falls.

The morning breaks; the steeds in their stalls

Stamp and neigh, as the hostler calls;

The day returns, but nevermore

Returns the traveler to the shore.

And the tide rises, the tide falls.

Katlynn also remembered something else her daddy told her. He had said, "At the beach, life is different as time doesn't move from hour to hour, but moment to moment. We live by the currents, plan by the tides and follow the sun."

Her thoughts were interrupted by the clinking of glasses as the owners raised a glass to cheer and to celebrate. Then they asked if anyone wanted to pray. Most everyone was caught off guard as they looked at each other. Katlynn had not talked to God in a long time; she did not know what to say. But Damian stood up and cleared his throat. He placed his hands on the shoulders of Maggie and Katlynn and began.

"Good and Gracious God, we thank you for gathering us here today and for all the gifts that you've given us in the year that's past. We welcome the new additions to this table like myself and my family as well as the guests who return every year. We are grateful for their presence, and bless all those responsible for the food we are about to eat. And we remember those who go without: without homes, without food, without peace. And those who lost a lot or everything in Hurricane Florence in North Carolina in September. We ask you to bless them and to soften our hearts. Amen."

Damian gave a small squeeze to Maggie and Katlynn's shoulders and sat down. Maggie looked over at Damian and said a whisper of thanks. Katlynn touched his leg and gave him a kiss on the cheek. Then the eating and laughing began. After the dessert was served a small basket full of notes of thanks were passed around. Most were about thankful for family, work, friends, Jesus, and health; a short sentence or two. Someone pulled out a long note and read it. He stood as he read, "I am thankful for the circumstances that I encounter; in a stranger I just met at an unexpected place; a family who has been always there but I just ignored because of my imperfect relationship with them; it might be a longtime friend I have or a friend I just met. I want to open my heart and see how blessed I am to have them all in my life. Sometimes they are the light that shines in my path in some dark phases of life." Then the man sat down. Everyone wondered who at the table wrote that, but no one asked.

Some people left to go back home. Some stayed and walked the trails around the property for exercise. Others saddled horses and rode the horse trail near the water. There were rocking chairs beside a roaring fire. Maggie took a cup of hot spiced tea and sat down. Damian came and sat beside her. Katlynn had gone to see the owners and to talk about the article. "Maggie, thank you for being with us today. I heard Sophia was out of town and I wanted you to be with me and Katlynn. I was not sure if Katlynn was coming at first," he laughed with truthfulness in his voice.

"Katlynn's life changed abruptly. She was thrown into a new situation and she was such a daddy's girl. I believe she has regrets that she did not tell Jim how much she loved him when he left us. But she was only a child. Not even I knew what the future would hold. It is just that I have my faith that has held me together all this time. I am not saying Katlynn does not have faith; please do not think I know what is in her heart. But I believe she has been running all of her life. Thank you for being such a good friend."

Damian scooted closer to Maggie. "I love her. I want to ask her to marry me, but I am afraid she will say no."

"Give her time. But on the other hand, life is too short. It can be gone in a moment. I wish I knew then what I know now. I would have practiced Corinthians Chapter 13. Even if Jim had still died, I would have felt better by him." Maggie took a sip of her tea.

Damian looked confused, so Maggie began to speak. "Love is patient, love is kind. It does not envy, it does not boast, it is not proud. It does not dishonor others, it is not self-seeking, it is not easily angered, and it keeps no record of wrongs. Love does not delight in evil but rejoices with the truth. It always protects, always trusts, always hopes, and always perseveres. Love never fails"

Maggie continued, "I was not patient with Jim when he decided to leave Wake Forest, NC and take over the family business. I was envious of his relationships with his family and longtime friends. I was so self-seeking and boy did I keep a record of wrongs. But I loved that man. He knew it, too."

Damian opened his wallet and pulled out a photo of Jim and Maggie. They were standing on the dock hand in hand watching the sunset sink into the water. They looked happy and in love to him. He handed it to Maggie.

"Where did you get this?" Maggie held it to her heart.

"From Bobby Harcourt. I met him while I was on assignment. He would love to see you and Katlynn. Said he tried to reach you at Sophia's but apparently she told him that you and your daughter were moving on and she thought it would not be a good idea." Damian wished he would not have told her that.

Maggie did not look surprised. "My grief was so great and I was trying to raise a teenage girl. But it was no excuse. I thought they would have blamed me for Jim's death. So, I just let the past be the past."

"Has Katlynn seen this? May I have it to keep?" Maggie was stilling holding on to the photo.

111

"You keep it. No, Katlynn does not know. The only ones I have is of her and Jim on the shrimping boat and one with her and an old black dog. I did show her those."

Katlynn walked up while Damian was kissing Maggie on the top of her head. She looked surprised and wondered what those two had been up to.

"Mama, I hope you had a great Thanksgiving. It was my best one yet. I could really get into this as a tradition," Katlynn said as she winked at Damian.

Maggie told them she was going to just sit by the fire and talk to some people and drink her tea. She encouraged them to go on a sleigh ride. She could see the man hitching two horses to a carriage. "Go on, now." She nodded at Damian.

The carriage man helped them up into the coach. He put the red horses' blanket over their laps. He took the reins and the horses began to trot. Katlynn laid her head on Damian's shoulder and closed her eyes. She told him what she heard and saw. He smiled and kissed her on the lips. Finally, Katlynn was becoming the person he always knew was deep inside. The new Katlynn he wanted to know more of. He loved the old Katlynn, too. But he wanted to see her grow in love and beauty that he heard was there when she was a little girl. Bobby had told him a lot about her.

When the ride was over, he took her into the stable to see the horses. As she patted the nose of a large brown horse with a white spot on his nose, it began to neigh and they both laughed as the horse stomped his feet. She stumbled and fell in the hay.

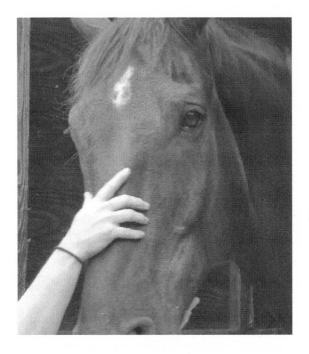

"Katlynn Harcourt, this is not where I had imagined I would be doing this." Damian got down on his knee.

He pulled out a velvet bag. In the velvet bag was a diamond ring that had belonged to his mother. It was a pear-shaped diamond.

"Katlynn, I love you. Will you marry me?" Damian was shaking. What if she said no? Or not yet. Or take me home. His palms were sweating.

Katlynn looked at him and got down on her knees. She flung her arms around him and said, "Yes. I will marry you." She knocked him off balance into the hay. They lay there in the hay laughing. He helped her up and brushed her off; then he brushed the hay off of himself. The velvet bag lay in the hay. He picked it up and opened the bag. He put the ring on her finger. It fit perfectly.

Maggie was still in the rocking chair when they returned. He put his arms around Maggie and said, "She said yes." Maggie stood up and hugged them both. Then they made their way back to New York and to North Carolina. This year was a lot to be thankful for, thought Maggie.

Chapter 11

Katlynn was in her office when Ella came through the door at an almost run. "Damian told me he asked you to marry him over Thanksgiving? Is this true? How did you keep this relationship a secret for so long?"

"Yes, he did. And it just kind of happened so fast. I cannot explain love, Ella. It is a mystery to me. I told him I want to get married in the spring or maybe in the summer. He wants to get married on December 23rd." Katlynn stood up and walked around to the front of her desk.

"December 23 of next year?" Ella questioned.

"No. Like in three weeks. How can we get everything ready in three weeks?" Katlynn looked stressed.

Ella leaned over and asked at an almost whisper, "Are you pregnant? I will not tell anyone."

"No!" Katlynn was shocked that Ella had asked such a question.

"Then what is the problem. Do you love him? Are you having second thoughts?" Ella sat down in the chair.

"No. I love him. But he wants a church wedding. How are we going to pull this off so close to Christmas? I have never planned a wedding; I hear there is a lot to do. I do not know where to begin."

Ella smiled. "Oh, you and Damian tell me what your wishes are. I am a master planner; a girl who loves details. I can make this happen."

Katlynn hugged her. "I will tell Damian tonight that I will agree to get married on December 23rd. We will be in touch."

That evening Damian and Katlynn talked of the wedding. He was relieved that she had agreed to get married so soon. He did not want to wait until spring. He was so in love with her. Maybe he was afraid she would back out. But he was ready to begin his life with her. He was young, but he had figured out early in life that life is too short. Working on the assignment after Hurricane Florence and meeting Katlynn's family had made him think about a lot of things. He missed his family; he wanted a family so badly. He learned from Bobby Harcourt that having somewhere to go is HOME, and having someone to love is FAMILY. And having both is a blessing. Katlynn's granddaddy had died years ago. No one told her because they did know where she was living. Her cousin had joined the Coast Guard long ago. He had told Bobby that he wanted to keep in touch; wanted him and whoever was left to be his family.

They both met with Ella the next morning. They gave her their wishes, the dollar amount to spend and told her they wanted a simple wedding. They wanted close friends and family; nothing really extravagant. Simple. They wanted simple. Ella took lots of notes. Her notebook was full of information after two days. She had a plan. Then she took Katlynn shopping. They flew to North Carolina one Saturday morning. Maggie met them at the airport. It was time to pick out the dress.

Maggie and Ella waited outside the dressing room. Katlynn came out with a long dress with a high neck and lots of lace. Katlynn turned around and around in the mirror with a smile on her face. Maggie and Ella both shook their heads "no." The dressing room clerk took her two more dresses. She came out and again they shook their heads "no." Katlynn sighed. Ella took the clerk aside and whispered in her ear. The clerk smiled and came back with another dress. This time Katlynn came out in a white A-line Princess V-neck asymmetrical lace dress. She had on a simple headband with lace and pearls. When Katlynn turned around to look in the mirror, she even gasped herself.

117

That dress was 'it.' She was absolutely stunning. They headed back to New York with dress in tow.

Ella took Lindsay and Hannah shopping next. In a little boutique just down from their office building were two dresses in the window. Both were green velvet and was the perfect size for both girls. Ella chose a black tux with red cummerbunds for Matt and Cameron and even for Damian. Matt and Cameron's ties were black as Damian's tie was red. They brought it back to the office to show Katlynn. She loved it. Ella kept busy for seven days planning; Damian and Katlynn approved of everything she chose.

Saturday December 22 was the rehearsal. The church was filled with red poinsettias in the front of the sanctuary. The window sills had holly with red berries and white candles that threw a glow against the stained-glass windows. On the right side of the church was a large Chrismon tree with white lights. On the left side where they were to stand was a manger scene. Pastor Sapp asked them if they wanted it moved. Damian told him no. He wanted Jesus right there in the wedding. Katlynn agreed.

On December 23rd Damian stood at the front of the church along with Pastor Sapp and listened as the piano played 'Here Comes the Bride.' He watched with tears in his eyes as she

118

walked down the aisle towards him. He had never seen her more beautiful than today. Pastor Sapp asked, "Who gives Katlynn away?" She had forgotten about that part of the ceremony. Ella had not mentioned anything in all of her notes and planning. Just as she began to worry Bobby walked toward her and stood beside her. He said, "Maggie and I" as he put her hand into Damian's. Then he sat down with Maggie. Katlynn whispered, "thank you." He nodded.

The pastor continued, "In the Holy Scriptures we are taught that marriage was instituted by God Himself, and is therefore a holy estate. According to the ordinance of God, a man and his wife shall be one flesh and that he should love her even as Christ also loved the Church. That they should love one another, be faithful one to the other, bear with each other's infirmities and weaknesses, cherish each other in all things and live together as heirs of the grace of life."

He asked them to commit to each other their vows. They both said, "I do." They each placed rings on each other's finger and kissed.

Damian held up Katlynn's hand and said, "This ring has no beginning or end and is therefore a symbol of infinity. It is endless, eternal, just the way love should be. I promise to each of you all in front of God that I will love her until death do we part and even after." The pastor pronounced them husband and wife.

At the reception they greeted guests as everyone entered the fellowship hall. The reception was the traditional Italian wedding reception. Damian had agreed with Ella to have the traditional American ceremony, but wanted his culture represented at the reception. Ella had kept this a secret from Katlynn, too, but she loved it. When the music began, they led their guests in the dance called La Tarantela; it is a dance where everyone holds hand and rotate clockwise. As the music speeds up they reverse. Katlynn had not had such fun.

Their cake was not the traditional American layered cake. Their cake was the Cassata Alla Siciliana, a traditional Italian Cheesecake served with wine. They partied almost till morning. They went back to the apartment. They would go on a formal honeymoon soon. But tonight, they relished in the day of friends, family and new love. On Christmas Eve Bobby and Maggie came over for breakfast. They all opened gifts and then Maggie and Bobby headed back to North Carolina. Damian and Katlynn would fly out to Italy on Christmas Day.

They landed in Florence, Italy and were taken by limousine to where they would be staying for three days. Damian had chosen a Bed and Breakfast called the Villa **Antea**. **It was a** fairy-tale type place within walking distance to Florence's historical city center. The room had antiques, period paintings, silk tapestries, and marble walls. He had an agenda in hand to follow. The first day they went to The Magnificent Uffizi Gallery museums. It houses some of the most important works of Leonardo da Vinci, Grotto, Botticelli and Michelangelo. They toured Casa di Dante to see the collection of poetry and writings of this famous author. They went to see the 311-foot-high bell tower of the Palazzo Vecchio Museum and Tower. The second day they took classes with Chefs Fiamma and Ginny where they learned to cook a complete Tuscan meal.

They ate at the Savini Tartufi Truffle restaurant, the La Piccola Corte and the Il Conventino a Marignolle.

The last day Damian took Katlynn shopping. They both bought a very formal piece of clothing. He was going to take her to the Cathedral called The Duomo. It is a 13th century church with beautiful frescoes. When they arrived, she knew why they were dressed as they were. There was a sign that said, "At this religious site wear appropriate respectable clothing. You will not be allowed inside wearing shorts, tank tops, sandals, hats or sunglasses." Katlynn thought, how unlike the typical American churches today.

Once inside after the tour Damian led Katlynn to the front of the church. Be pulled out some slips of paper from his inside jacket pocket. They sat down on the altar. He said it was tradition for five people to give him marital advice. Five people had slipped him these messages in a small mason jar right after the wedding reception. He wanted to share with her now, he said.

Never both be angry at the same time.
Never yell at each other unless the house is on fire.
Neglect the whole world rather than each other.
Never go to sleep with an argument unsettled.
When you are wrong, be ready to admit and ask for forgiveness.

Katlynn took his hand and gave it a kiss. With tears in her eyes she said that was great advice for both of them. The faith she had as a little child began to seep into her veins again. She pondered them in her heart.

Their time was up in Italy. It was time to go back to the United States and begin their life together.

Chapter 12

Matt came into Katlynn's office and asked if it was a good time for him to talk to her. He was requesting to go back to North Carolina, Harkers Island in particular, to do a follow up of the aftermath of Hurricane Florence. Katlynn did not answer right away. She looked out the window at the New York skyline and thought about Florence. One Florence was in Italy and was the most beautiful place she had ever seen. If she could imagine Heaven, she thought it may look like that. Then she thought about Florence the hurricane. How one to three days of weather can destroy property, land and life. What a contrast. She had almost forgotten Matt was standing there when he cleared his throat.

"I am sorry, Matt. I was just thinking," as she turned around to look at him.

He came over to her and put his hand on her shoulder. "Damian told me about your family in Harkers Island. I am sorry I did not know all that when we went there the first time on assignment. I learned about it when we got back."

"It is okay. It is something that I did not share. It was something that I tried to run away from. I guess I did not run far enough away. I guess running away will not change anything if you are running away from yourself." Katlynn looked at Matt somberly.

"I want Damian to go back with me. And I want you to go too, Katlynn. That is if you want to go. Most stories that I report on is a job; I get the facts and move on. But I have been following the story of the recovery for months by looking at everything I can get my hands on. I want to see firsthand the recovery and progress for myself. There is something about that place." Matt went to the window and looked out at the gray sky. The buildings were half hidden by the fog.

"I will ask if they will let us all go and get back to you. Yes, I would love to go. Maybe I can handle it now since they are on the road to recovery." Katlynn watched as he left the office and shut her door. Recovery. What is recovery? The definition is the restoration to a former or better condition. She liked the better condition part most.

Katlynn's mind began to open up and create again. She wrote down on the pad on her desk these thoughts. 'Recovery begins at exactly that moment when you are completely broken to pieces and must surrender to unfamiliar and uncomfortable ways in order to rebuild into who you were meant to be.' She then wrote, 'I am going to make the rest of my life the best of my life.' She talked to her boss and then called Damian and

Matt. They were going to be on the next plane to North Carolina.

They arrived in New Bern, NC and took a rental car to Harkers Island. This was exciting for Katlynn. She had forgotten how much fun it was to be back in the field instead of behind the desk. Matt interviewed farmers still trying to recover from the massive flooding. He spoke to fishermen who lost their livelihood; he spoke with people still needing their house repaired, and business people. He learned that 42 people lost their lives and there were 17 billion dollars in damage. He learned of the progress for small business owners who applied for low interest loans and long-term disaster loans for physical damage and working capital. He spoke with people who received disaster unemployment assistance for work impacted by the storm. FEMA representatives told him that 1,024 people were checked into hotels and were getting help with costs from the Shelter Assistance Programs. 355 FEMA travel trailers had been installed for those who lost their homes; those whose homes were totally destroyed with no hopes of repairs. He learned that help came from the National Guard soldiers, State Troopers, 14 Swift Water Rescue Teams, 28 Boat Crews and help from other states along with assistance from local churches and non-profit organizations. Matt heard over and over the quote of "Carteret Strong."

126

Katlynn watched and listened as Damian interviewed local people as he stopped the car and went into the yards and homes of random folks. He learned of loss; not the loss that can be replaced by money and things. Real loss such as the old love letters from a husband who had not come back from the Korean War, the old wedding dresses boxed and placed into attics, old photographs (the ones that cannot be replaced), Christmas ornaments that have been collected over the years, a box of arrowheads and other collections.

They had spent 12 hours interviewing and taking photos. They were all tired and Matt drove as they headed back to the hotel when Katlynn yelled, "Stop! Pull over."

Matt did as she said. Damian asked, "What is it honey? What is wrong?"

Katlynn explained that she thought that was the place she had grown up. She asked Matt to pull into the driveway. She opened the car door to get out and Matt and Damian were going to follow when she asked them to stay in the car. Katlynn approached the house and carefully rang the doorbell. A young woman with a child on her hip answered the door. She did not open the screen door all the way as she looked at two men in a car in her driveway and a young woman on her porch.

"May I help you?" the young woman asked.

"I grew up here. May I look around?" Katlynn asked as she watched the woman's face.

"You must be mistaken. My husband and I bought this piece of property years ago. It was an empty lot except for the Fishing House on the property. The dock was damaged from a hurricane so we moved it over four feet. We built this house. You must be mistaken." The woman began to close the door when Katlynn began to beg.

"I thought if I could just walk around this place and feel it that this brokenness inside me might start healing. If you will let me please go into the Fish House and walk around, I swear I will not take anything but a memory." Katlynn's heart began to beat a little faster.

"No, you must be mistaken. It must be some other place you are thinking about. You need to leave." The woman shut the screen door and locked it. The child began to cry.

"Please, mam," Katlynn replied. "I had carved my name and Rascals into the wood on the wall of that little Fish House. It is where I did my homework and where Rascal and I played. I am lost in this old world and forgot who I am. I swear I will not take anything. Please."

"Are you Katlynn?" the woman asked. "Katlynn and Rascal is carved on the wall. Rascal is buried out behind the house under the Yaupon tree. We have left the grave maker all these years. Go ahead, but do not be long." The woman shut the door. She heard it click as she walked off the porch.

Damian rolled down the window and asked if everything was okay. She told him to stay in the car; she would be back in a moment. Katlynn opened the door to the Fish House. It was like her daddy had left it; like nothing had been touched in years. It is odd how a hurricane can destroy a house to splinters and yet a Fish House or other structure on the same property can stand. She took her finger and traced her and Rascal's name on the wall. She closed the door. She could see the woman look out her window at her. She went into the backyard and there under the Yaupon Tree was grass neatly mowed and yet there were two wooden sticks in the shape of a cross. It was where Rascal was buried.

Katlynn then walked out onto the dock as the woman was still watching her. She took off her shoes and put her toes into the water. She closed her eyes and could smell and taste the salt air; she could see and taste her childhood. She carried her shoes and stopped one more time at the grave and blew a kiss to Rascal. She made her way to the car and told Matt and Damian it was time to go back to the hotel. On the way to the hotel she yelled, "Stop" again.

Matt pulled into a parking lot of an old white wooden church. The sign said ALL WELCOME! THIS SUNDAY COME AND HAVE DINNER ON THE GROUNDS FOLLOWED BY A BAPTISM AFTERWARDS. Matt looked at Daman and said, "It looks like we need to go shopping. We are going to church in the morning." They both smiled.

They entered the church and sat towards the back. Damian had told her long ago that she had forgotten how to hear and see. She closed her eyes to see if she still could. In her mind

131

she smelled her mama's Jergens lotion and Juicy Fruit Chewing Gum and her daddy's Old Spice Aftershave. She was back in time, sitting between her parents and feeling safe when she heard the preacher ask if anyone felt the call to come to Jesus and be baptized. She opened her eyes and walked towards the front of the church. Matt and Damian watched as the preacher spoke softly to her in private. She nodded her head.

The congregation gathered around the banks of the water as the Preacher, wearing a black suit and tie and a white towel around his neck took off his socks and shoes and waded into the water. Katlynn was wearing a sundress and sandals. She took off her sandals and waded into the water. The people began to sing the familiar hymn *Shall We Gather at the River* by Robert Lowry.

"Shall we gather at the river, where bright angel feet have trod, with its crystal tide forever, flowing by the throne of God? Yes, we'll gather at the river, the beautiful, beautiful, river; gather with the saints at the river that flows by the throne of God."

He led her into the cold water and held his hand up to God and said, "I baptize you in the name of the Father, the Son and the Holy Ghost." Then he took her body and pushed her under the water.

He then pulled her up, wiped her face with the towel and led her back to the banks where the people of God were waiting. They began to sing again.

"Ere we reach the shining river, lay we every burden down; grace our spirits will deliver, and provide a robe and crown."

The people continued to sing. Katlynn had gone under the water as a young woman and came up as a new person with death to sin and her new life in Christ. The people gathered all around her, hugging her and singing one last song.

"There is a river and it flows from deep within. There is a fountain that frees the soul from sin. Come to the water, there is vast supply. There is a river that never shall run dry."

One of the women in the church came up to Katlynn and put her arms around her. "Are you Jim Harcourt's daughter? You resemble him a lot. He was a member of this church."

Katlynn answered, "Yes, he was my daddy."

"Well welcome back, dear. Life takes you to unexpected places, but love brings you home." She then walked away into the crowd.

Then Matt, Damian and Katlynn headed back to New York, but taking a part of Harkers Island with them all.

Chapter 13

Katlynn looked up from her desk and realized it was dark outside. She looked at the time on her phone; 8 pm. Riding through the drive thru at McDonalds she ordered a burger and fries. Damian had gone out into the field again for an assignment. He had been gone for 3 weeks this time. She pulled into the parking space in front of the apartment. Then she saw Damian's car. She had forgotten he was coming home today. She opened the door and could smell something good to eat. At the kitchen table was Damian with two places set and lighted candles. He looked up at her with her bag in her hand. He said nothing. He proceeded to warm up dinner in the microwave. On the table was three weeks' worth of mail. Under his placemat she noticed an envelope, turned upside down. He set the warm plates of food down and motioned for her to sit.

Immediately she began to apologize. She put the paper bag on the table beside where she sat down. Damian still said nothing. Katlynn began again, "I am so sorry! I know you told me that you were coming home. I just got caught up at the office and the time got away from me again." She took a bite of her food and savored the bite.

Damian looked at her hard and began. "Katlynn, Ella told me you worked 14-hour days again while I was gone. And I can see from the bag of burgers and fries that you have not been eating well. I am worried about your health. Not just your physical health, but your mental." He stood and took his plate to the sink and rinsed it and put it in the dishwasher.

"Oh, Damian, do not be so hard on me. You know how much work it is to be Editor in Chief; and how much work it took to get there." Katlynn ate the last bite and took her plate to the sink. He took it from her.

"Katlynn, it looks like all you have done since I left was work. You did not even get the mail out of the box." Pointing to the pile on the table he continued, "There is three weeks' worth here. Two bills are going to be past due." He turned and left the kitchen. She followed.

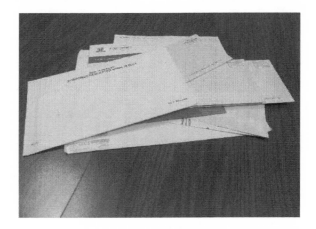

"Are you mad at me? Is this our first fight?" Katlynn raised her voice.

Damian quietly sat in the recliner and said, "No, Katlynn. You would be better off if it was our first fight. I am not angry at you. Just the opposite. Something has to give."

Katlynn replied, "What do you mean something has to give?"

Damian stood up and took her hand. He led her to the couch and put his arms around her. "I love you. My outlook on life changed after visiting Harkers Island. Didn't it yours? Did you not feel a sense of community and the freedom and quietness of a slow lifestyle? Did you not notice that people actually spent time with each other? That they had time for each other and their neighbors? Here in New York I feel like I am on a hamster wheel. I used to love it here; the plays, the fast days, the opportunities and the feel of the city. Now that I got a taste of family my priorities have changed."

"But our life and jobs are here," Katlynn said with eyebrows furrowed. She could not imagine leaving the city, although she did feel calm in her soul at her childhood home. She had been away so long; and she could not remember much about that place. Most of her memories were made in Wake Forest, NC where she grew into a teenager and young woman.

Damian went to the table and came back with an envelope. He folded it and put it in his front shirt pocket. Katlynn watched as he did this; it was like he was hiding something or putting something close to his heart. She was good at observations and facts; she had studied it and breathed it most of her adult life. Everything had to be analyzed by her. Black and white. Her world was black and white.

Katlynn took his hand into hers. She rubbed his fingers and looked him in the eyes. He had no expression. This concerned her. "Damian, what is that in your pocket?"

"Do you really want to know? I do not know if I want to share it right now. I may just throw it away." He seemed upset by the moment.

"No, Damian, I want to know. Are they divorce papers?" She had a panic in her voice.

Damian held her tight. "No, Katlynn. I love you. This is an offer letter." He pulled it out of his pocket and straightened it out.

"Offer letter?" Katlynn looked confused.

"Yes, Katlynn. It is an offer letter. I applied for a job as a Professor in the English Department teaching Journalism at

Duke University. They have offered me the position. I have already had a telephone interview. They want to meet me in person and for me to accept and complete the paperwork."

Katlynn looked more confused. "I did not know that you were looking for a job; especially a job in North Carolina. Did it occur to you to share that with me? What about my career, Damian?"

"Katlynn, if we both happen to be home at the same time then maybe we could talk. But I have been gone three weeks and you did not even remember that your husband was coming home. I am going to take a shower and go to bed."

Katlynn watched as he left the room. She heard the shower turn on. She laid face down on the couch and began to cry. She thought, "Damian is right. We have only been married a few months and he is gone most of the time; and I am working late again. My work is my husband. And my husband is in the shower and is going to bed. He does not even want to talk to me."

She looked up on the book shelf and saw the Mason jar from their wedding. It had dust on the lid. Had it been that long since they looked at it? She blew the top and dust flew into the air. She sneezed. She opened the jar and put her hand in it and pulled out one of the papers.

It read, "Never go to sleep with an argument unsettled." Damian had stepped out of the shower and was drying off with a towel when Katlynn entered the bathroom with the slip of paper in her hand.

He put the towel around his waist and smiled; a little smile, but a smile at least, thought Katlynn. "What do you have in your hand?"

"Go get your sweat pants on and come to the living room. We have to talk."

Damian met her on the couch; she showed him the note. He kissed her passionately. They talked about family, their goals,

140

hopes and dreams. She thought about what her mama had said on how she wished she had embraced change instead of fighting it. She did not want to make the same mistake. But she was scared. Damian said he agreed with her. And yes, it is scary to make changes. Especially radical life style and location changes. Then her husband said something profound. He said, "Making a big life change is pretty scary, Katlynn, but you know what is even scarier to me?" Katlynn watched the seriousness in his eyes.

"What is even scarier?" she asked.

"Regret."

Katlynn understood what he was saying. She had lived with regrets all her life. Regrets that she was not able to go back to the house and bring some special things with her, regret that she did not realize it was going to be the last time she saw her daddy and regret that she did not tell him how much she loved him, regret that she had shut out her mama, Aunt Sophia and others who tried to help her along the way and regret that she had held on to such anger and hurt towards God. How much love and opportunities to grow had she missed all these years? If not for her mild heart attack she would have missed loving Damian and being married. It had made her slow down and take stock of her life.

"Damian, I do not want to regret anymore. Tell me about this job. How do you see our life together in the future?"

Damian began. "I miss you like crazy when I am gone into the field. I do not even have the passion anymore to focus on what the story should be. Like I said earlier, I feel like a hamster on a wheel and cannot get off. I was surfing the internet and found a job posting for Duke University. I have my PhD in English and have been a journalist for a long time. They want someone who has experience out in the field and someone who would love to mentor college age students. When I read the job description my heart began to race with enthusiasm. I have not had such enthusiasm in a very long time. It was like a spark of something new and important. Something that I could make a difference in."

Katlynn could see something in him she had never seen before. But where would they live? How about her career? What would she do?

Damian continued, "I spoke with the Associate Provost and he said we could live in the faculty apartments which does not cost very much. So, we could make it on my salary living there. I would be near my colleagues and students. It would be fun being back on a campus with all the energy young people bring to the table. I feel like you can take a much-needed break;

142

maybe even begin that book you have been always talking about writing but never had time. But most importantly, we can be near family. Especially when we have children of our own."

Katlynn nodded. It would be nice. How fortunate she was to have a man who wanted to be near her family; who loved family and knew the importance of those relationships. She had taken her mama and Aunt Sophia for granted all these years. Damian had lost all of his family to deaths; she had not even thought about that for herself. She could be alone like him. She shuddered at the thought.

"Damian, go to the interview. Feel out to see if this is what you really want to do. If it feels right come back home and we both will turn in our notice at work."

"Katlynn, I love you more than you will ever know." Damian picked up the phone and made the arrangements to come to North Carolina for the interview.

Katlynn took him to the airport and watched as the plane took off with her husband. Seeing him go once more made her long for him; she was missing him already. She closed her eyes and breathed deeply. The thought came to her mind. And suddenly she knew that it was time to start something new and trust the magic of new beginnings. Sometimes things happen. Unexpected ones. And it changes your life in an instant. All your prayers, all your problems, and all the things that once bothered you before, all the things you thought were unsolvable just dissolve and vanish away in an instant like smoke. You cannot even pinpoint when and where it all happened or the specific moment or event that marks the change. But for some reason, you know without a doubt that you are now standing on the after of before.

Damian called her late that night. It felt right and true. He accepted the job. They both turned in their notice at work. Damian worked his two-week notice and moved into the apartment at Duke University. Katlynn had to give a month's notice because of her position. On her last day of work, she watched as the men took her packed boxes to her car. Roger, the building superintendent, came into her office. He wished her well in her new adventure. Then he looked up at her wall of pictures he had hung on her first day at work. He saw the new photo that was in the empty space where he had put a hanger. He studied the photo. He turned to Katlynn and said, "A daddy holds his daughter's hand for a short while, but he holds her heart forever." He carefully removed the picture, wrapped it and handed it to her. Then he gave her a slight kiss on the head and walked out. She followed behind him, getting on the elevator one last time and walked out into the sunlight. It is not about letting go; it is about taking everything you thought is true and throwing it out the window. It is about embracing life's unpredictability and letting go of boundaries and starting over. With her car packed full she headed toward the highway and to her new beginning.

Chapter 14

Katlynn put in her new address into the GPS. It led her up a tree lined hill to a set of red brick apartments. She parked her car in the spot beside Damian's car, turned off the engine and sat there for a moment taking it all in. 'Do not panic, she thought to herself. This is going to be a new experience. Open your mind and heart to this; do not be like Maggie and be resentful. This new adventure is something that Damian really wants. You will find your way, too.' She looked up and saw the front door open. Damian rushed out to meet her as she got out of the car. He carried her over the threshold of their new home. He sat her down when they stepped inside. Katlynn looked around at her surroundings. The living room had bookshelves against one whole wall; the couch was a light blue with matching floral chairs.

The coffee table was out of brown walnut wood. The kitchen overlooked the living room; it was divided by a bar only. A small table for two sat in the corner near a window that overlooked a grassy area. Some college aged kids were throwing a football. The bathroom was small with only a shower. The bedroom was the biggest room in the house. The walls were white as was the whole apartment. No art hung on the walls. The second bedroom had been made into an office. Damian had set up two desks in the room each facing the opposite wall. The whole place looked like it needed a good paint job and some major decorating. She tried to be hopeful, but Damian could see it in her face.

"Katlynn, you will love it here. I have met most of our neighbors. What do you think?"

She thought for a moment and took a deep breath. She remembered how her mama had been and did not want to repeat that mistake. "It is smaller than our New York apartment. Did you buy the furniture or did it come furnished?"

"No, it came furnished. They did say we could add art to the walls if needed. But we have to keep the furniture. But I have not been here much except to sleep. After classes I have been working in the Library." Damian had excitement in his voice.

147

Katlynn could hear his enthusiasm and hope in his voice. "I am sure it will be fine. It has been a long ride. Let's unpack the car and let me get a good night's sleep. Then I can explore in the morning."

Katlynn must have overslept as she rolled over and Damian was gone. She saw a note on the bedside table saying he would be out of class at 4:00. She rubbed her eyes and sat up. Today she would spend the day unpacking and decorating this place. She was determined to make this place a home. She took pictures with her phone of each room and took off towards the shops. It took 3 hours to purchase what she needed. The walls were white; she knew she could not paint them so she had to be creative. She purchased soft burlap looking coverlets for the couch and the two chairs to cover the blue and floral designs. Pillows of light green were then placed on the couch and chairs. A green plant in a white and brown pot was put on the coffee table along with some candles. She chose art with trees and meadows for the wall in the living room. On the small table for two that sat in the corner she placed a green gingham tablecloth; white bows were tied to the back of the chairs to carry the theme in the open floor plan.

The walls in their bedroom were white as well. She chose a navy blue and white bedspread with an assortment of matching pillows. She placed photos of her and Damian in silver plated picture frames on the wall and on the night stands. A tall green cactus was placed in the corner near the window that gave light to the room. In their office she placed some pottery, photos and a couple of plants on the bookshelves. She stood back to look at each room and was pleased.

The landing outside the door was concrete and very small. She had found an old wooden cane chair and a small table. On the table she placed a pot of colorful flowers. It made the apartment look more inviting. One of her neighbors came over and commented on the work she had done.

Right at 4:00 as Damian had said she saw him coming across the grass, briefcase in hand. She ran to meet him. She took his hand in hers and they walked in silence to the apartment. When he saw what she had done to the outside he smiled. Once he opened the door and went inside, he could not believe it was the same place!

"Katlynn, I cannot believe this is our apartment. You have done an excellent job of decorating. Not only are you beautiful, but you are talented and smart." He gave her a big kiss and went to sit down on the couch. She told him about her shopping; he told her about his day. Today he had introduced a new contemporary poet by the name of Kelli Russell

Agodon. He liked her poetry. She was from Seattle, Washington, he said.

"It sounds interesting, Damian. Could I come tomorrow and audit your class? I promise I will not do this every day; I know it will be a conflict of interest, but I would really like to do something to stimulate my mind." Katlynn watched his face for a response.

"I do not see why not. One time would not hurt. You could talk to the Dean to see what you would need to do if you wanted to audit other classes on campus."

"That is a great idea. I had not thought of that. I will make an appointment in the morning. But may I still come to hear you teach just this once?" Katlynn asked pleadingly.

"Of course, but we need to keep this professional. The other students do not need to know you are my wife for now."

"Understood," said Katlynn.

Damian's class began at 10:00 a.m. She stood outside in the hallway as she saw the students make their way to their seats. Once all were seated, she took an empty chair at the back of the room. He projected the poem onto the board.

Of a Forgetful Sea by Kelli Russell Agodon

Sometimes, I forget the sun

sinking into ocean.

Desert is only a handful of sand

held by my daughter.

In her palm,

she holds small creatures,

tracks an ant, a flea

moving over each grain.

She brings them to places

she thinks are safe:

an island of driftwood,

the knot of a blackberry bush,

a continent of grass.

Fire ants carried on sticks,

potato bugs scooped

into the crease of a newspaper.

She tries to help them

before the patterns of tides

reach their lives.

She knows about families

who fold together like hands,

a horizon of tanks moving forward.

Here war is only newsprint.

How easy it is not to think about it

as we sleep beneath our quiet sky,

slip ourselves into foam, neglectful

waves appearing endless.

    Katlynn listened as Damian prompted his students to dissect the poem apart.

A memory came to her mind. She could recall how she tried to help the smallest of animals get away from the water before the tide took them away; she could not help but wonder how they did not know that if they stayed, they would be killed by the water.

And yet everyday there were more and more to save. It was never ending. The poem was talking about war in another land, but she saw it as families staying huddled together while hurricanes came toward them; and yet they stayed and waited for the water and winds to take them along with the tide. Katlynn began to breathe heavily. She had slept beneath the quiet sky in Wake Forest, NC, while her daddy and Rascal stayed right at the tides edge. The water had taken them away, just like all the small creatures she had tried to save.

Damian's students were raising their hands and discussing war and more analogies of the poem while Katlynn slipped out the door. He was so engrossed in his teaching that he did not see her leave. Once outside she began to run. She ran up the grassy hill towards the apartment; and yet she kept on running. She ran until she was completely out of breath and her heart was pounding. She threw herself on the ground and for the first time she cried long sobbing, grief cries. The cries she had suppressed all of these years. She cried until she could cry no more. She had been running all this time; but for the first time since her daddy had died, she let all the emotions of grief, sorrow and deep love flow.

She rolled over and looked at the sky. Then she closed her eyes. Damian had accused her of not hearing and seeing sometimes. He was right. She shut her eyes tight and came to realize that running away from her problems was a race she would never win. Anyone could run away. That is super easy. But facing problems and working through them is what makes you strong. She had been running and running trying to catch up with something and all she had done was to go farther and farther away from the precious love that had been waiting for her all this time. It was the love of her mom, the love of Aunt Sophia, and she had almost missed the love of Damian and she had missed the love of a God who had been there waiting for

154

her to return. Katlynn sat up, wiped her face and stretched her body. It was time to stop running away and running toward what she wanted. It was time to find what she wanted. It would be a journey only she could travel. The steps she needed to take would be steps alone. It would be the only way to figure out where she needed to be.

She did talk to the Dean of the University. He suggested that she think about which classes to audit. He did not want her to just be in a class for fun. He wanted her to go home and think about a particular subject and focus on that. When Damian came home from work, he found her baking in the kitchen. She had on a pink apron.

"Something smells extra good. I am usually the cook and baker," he said as he put his arms around her waist. She smelled good.

"I am taking over the kitchen. Hot chocolate cookies will be out of the oven in a moment. Pour us both a glass of milk, please." Katlynn opened the oven and put the hot cookies on the rack. She put three on each plate and joined him at the table.

"What did you think of my class? I turned my back to the wall for a moment and you were gone." He touched her hand.

"It was lovely. I went to the Dean and he suggested that I concentrate on another subject; one that I can focus on what my interests are." She waited for his reply.

"Poetry too much for a girl who likes facts, huh?" He said jokingly.

"No, it was very meaningful and I got a whole lot out of it. But I think I want to audit classes on Environmental Science. It is something that I know a little about, but not a lot. So, I want to learn more." Katlynn did not want to talk to him about how the poem ripped her heart and yet it made her think and move on. This was a journey she would have to travel alone.

"I know one of the professors in that field. He is open than most for people to audit." Damian took a bite of cookie, the hot chocolate dripped on his shirt.

Katlynn laughed and handed him a napkin. "Let's go for an evening walk. I found a little cafe near campus. I want us to go out for a change of scenery. I feel like being outside tonight."

The next day Katlynn took a seat toward the front of the class on Environmental Science and Oceanography. The professor asked if anyone knew what the class was going to be about. Some raised their hands. He told them that this would include the study of weather, ocean currents, and sea life, and every other topic associated with the ocean. He described how important this field of study was because 70% on the earth was made up of water. They would spend lots of time conducting research, which means reading many pages of studies, running experiments, collecting data, and then writing about their results and sharing their findings with the world. Lots of this work will be done in the laboratory, but in order to study the ocean, they would spend time in the water, on the water, or near the water. Duke University has a building and laboratory in Beaufort, NC. They would go periodically there for class. By the end of the semester they would be able to use predictive computer models to describe various oceanic factors and how they may respond to climate change, prepare technical reports; publish research results and present research at seminars, conferences, and lectures for national and international stakeholders. Not all, he explained, but some may even be given the opportunity to consult with policymakers regarding relevant developments in oceanography.

Katlynn's adrenaline was going. She had found her passion. She was not sure what all this meant, but for the first time in a long, long time she felt the hand of God moving her forward. She knew in her heart that was where she was supposed to be. She could not wait to tell Damian.

He was so happy to see her this way. He had known all along that his wife, although beautiful and smart, had so much hidden talent in her just bursting to be released. He was her number one cheerleader.

Damian spoke with her professor one evening at a faculty meeting. He told him a little about Katlynn and asked that he keep it confidential, but he wanted to let him know that this professional journalist grew up around the water. She was ripe for learning and absorbing. He said he understood.

Katlynn's professor asked Damian if he and his wife would attend a retirement dinner for Professor Tilley, a former professor of Oceanography. They were delighted. The retirement dinner was a formal sit-down affair. After the meal they went to a room for drinks and desserts where they were to mingle. Damian had found another English professor to talk to. Katlynn was coming back from the ladies' room and went over to the punch bowl. Professor Tilley began to speak to her. He asked her name and what she taught.

"Oh, I am not a professor. I am here with my husband," she replied.

"Do you have a name? He peered over his glasses at her." He smiled and watched as she squirmed.

"Yes, my name is Katlynn Davito. I am auditing a class on Environment Science and Oceanography."

He pulled his glasses up on his nose. "I have never seen a blonde Italian before."

"I am not Italian," she laughed. "My husband Damian is. My maiden name was Harcourt. You do not find many Harcourts around here."

He moved closer to her face as if he was studying it. This made her uncomfortable and she took a step back. He apologized for being rude. But he had to ask her something. If she did not want to answer that would be okay, too.

"What is it?" Katlynn's stance was on the offensive.

"I had a young man in my class the first year of my teaching. A smart young man. He was the only student that I had who I recommended to go to Raleigh to work in the government. I felt he could make some major changes for North Carolina. It was a shame, I heard, when he left that job and went back home. His name was James Harcourt, but we called him Jim. I do not know what ever happened to that young man."

Katlynn was about to answer when another professor interrupted and took his attention away. She slowly left the area and went to find Damian. Now she knew why she was here. She found her answer. The famous quote by Pablo Picasso says, "The meaning of life is to find your gift. The purpose of life is to give it away." She and Damian walked hand in hand under the stars in silence, enjoying the evening back to their home.

Chapter 15

Katlynn and Damian got up early each day to have breakfast with each other; to have some quiet time before both of their hectic days began. Damian was working on a special project for the department along with his classes which was taking up a lot of his time. It was okay with Katlynn as she was so immersed in her auditing classes.

She was also spending time with Maggie and Aunt Sophia. Damian had encouraged her to build those relationships; he said it had been too long and life is too short. Looking at Aunt Sophia, who was six years older than her mama, she could tell she was slowing down. Relationships are like building a house. If you do not build it well it will collapse. She had spent too many years away, running away, to concentrate on what matters most at the end of the day. If Aunt Sophia had not interfered and stuck her nose in where it did not belong, she and Maggie would have had a relationship with the Harcourts that were left in Harkers Island. But she had and she was still trying to get over it. But Katlynn was beginning to rethink that. Relationships can get stronger when both are willing to understand mistakes and forgive each other. It was amazing how forgiving Maggie **was**. She wished she had her mama's traits. She and Damian had talked in lengths about this. He was

161

so wise. He told her that a relationship is not built on a length of time you have spent together, but it is based on the foundation you built together. He reminded her that you cannot look back. You have to look forward.

She wondered how Bobby Harcourt could forgive. Once he found out that it was not Maggie who was the one keeping Katlynn away, he forgave her. He said it was not her fault. Forgiveness. Uncle Bobby had deep faith like her daddy. She asked him after the wedding in private how he could just forget what Aunt Sophia had done. He told her he was working on it. But mostly he forgave Maggie because she did not know what her sister had done and it was not her fault. The bible says, "Bear with each other and forgive one another if any of you has a grievance against someone. Forgive as the Lord forgave you." Katlynn still had trouble wrapping her mind around that.

But could or would Aunt Sophia go with them to Harkers Island? She wanted them both to go with her when she would go soon for her class. She wanted to spend time with both of these women. She had not approached her yet. Aunt Sophia had taken over and was mean to the Harcourts, she heard, when they tried to reach out. I am sure she thought it was for their own good, but it was not her decision to make; it was Maggie's and she did not get that opportunity. Hippocrates once said, "Healing is a matter of time, but it is sometimes also a matter of opportunity." Maybe she would ask them both to come to Harkers Island with her. They could all stay with the Research Team in the RV. And they could go see Uncle Bobby while they were there.

At dinner that evening she told her ideas to Damian. He listened intently. She loved that about him. He always waited for her to finish talking before he spoke. "Katlynn, you can ask them both to go. But you cannot control what happens. Do not be disappointed if it turns out not what you thought it would be. But be open."

She called her mama and invited her to come with her. Maggie was excited to go back to Harkers Island and to be with her daughter. Katlynn called Aunt Sophia. She began to make excuses, but Katlynn persisted so she agreed to go. They all went in the Research Team van together. It was engaging to hear them all talk on the way down. It took a little over four hours to get to Harkers Island. They unloaded their gear and all moved into their RV for the week.

The next day Aunt Sophia and Maggie stayed in the camp and relaxed and went on walks while Katlynn went out with the Research Team. This time the team was studying Oysters. The team was gathering data on the decline of oysters in the NC waters. So far, the research showed issues with natural disasters that had major effects on them; unsuitable water quality, shellfish diseases, and the over-harvesting of oysters.

According to the data that had been gathered in 1902 800,000 bushels of oysters were harvested out of North Carolina waters. In 2017 that number was down to 158,000 bushels. Most of the students in class were wading into the waters. Since she was auditing the class she chose to watch and take notes.

Later that day Katlynn was walking around the edge of the water and saw a shrimping boat. She watched as they came to dock. Once the boat stopped, she asked if she could come aboard. They were skeptical at first. Then she pulled out the photo of her and Jim and they understood. She asked them if she could go out with them in the morning. A man named Bear told her to be there at 3:30am.

When she told Maggie, she was furious with her. "Young lady, do you not know how dangerous this is? You have no idea who these men are!"

Aunt Sophia chimed in. "We would rather you call Uncle Bobby if you want to go out on a boat."

But Katlynn said she needed to go with strangers; she had done risky before and nothing had ever happened. She had made up her mind.

Being on deck at 3:30 am was a bit early, but the rest of Bear's crew was already there. The motor was running and nets and chains were being repaired. There was still some lingering wind and rough water as they left the docks. The outside temperature was 43F as they pulled out and the water temperature was 63F. The crew informed her that the best shrimping starts once the water temperature reached 70 degrees F.

On the shrimp boat there was a large circular net on each side of the boat. In front of this net was a "door" that ran along the bottom and to scare critters up and into the following net. The circular net openings on the big nets had metal bars across them to prevent sea turtles from being netted. Then there was a smaller net with a door and the same configuration called a Try Net that was used to sample what was being caught in each area. The Try Net was pulled up every 20-30 minutes. The rule of thumb used was for every shrimp caught in the Try Net, there should be one pound of shrimp in the big nets and this determined when the big nets were pulled out of the water.

Bear put Katlynn at the sorting table. It was the safest place for her to be. Jellyfish covered the bottom of the sorting table the first time the nets were dumped. The shrimp were gathered and the rest of the sea life was returned to the ocean.

Once they got back to land, they had to prepare an order for a restaurant that requested 100 pounds of headless shrimp. Everyone else was able to work their way using two hands popping the heads off of a pile of shrimp, but it was not a skill that was easily acquired. Katlynn's pile of headless shrimp was only about one third of everyone else's by the time they were done working their way through the pile.

Once that job was done it took another two hours to get the boat back in shape and prepared for the next days' work. Katlynn was exhausted. She got back to the RV, showered and went to bed. Every bone and muscle in her body ached. She asked the professor if she could not go out in the field the next day. He agreed. So, Katlynn, Maggie and Aunt Sophia took one of the cars available and rode around the area. They came to a thrift store and pulled into the parking lot. It was a two-story house. Maggie and Katlynn went in. Aunt Sophia sat down on the steps going up to the porch.

"I hope you do not mind, but I would just like to sit while you two shop." Sophia stretched her legs into the yard.

"We may be awhile. Come on in you feel like it. We will meet on the porch when everyone is done." Maggie opened the door and Katlynn went in first. As Sophia was sitting there, the sun warming her face; a man got out of a blue pickup truck and began to walk up the sidewalk. He stopped suddenly. It was Bobby Harcourt.

"Fancy meeting you here, Sophia. What brings you to our detestable little town? Isn't that what you called it? If I am not mistaken when I called and tried to speak to Maggie after Jim died you would not let me speak to her. And you had the nerve to have him sent to Wake Forest, North Carolina. None of us even attended his funeral. You did not even let us know when his service was. And how granddaddy wanted to see Katlynn before he died. I called the phone number and it had been changed to a non-published number. And here you are."

Bobby stood over her, looking down at her. Sophia did not look up. She stared at her feet. She could feel his breath on the top of her head.

Bobby continued. "We missed seeing our niece grow up. We missed being there for Maggie. We all were hurt so badly. Jim should have been buried in our family graveyard out back of the property."

Sophia still did not look up. Everything he was saying was true.

"You once had a lot to say. What is it, Sophia? What do you have to say now? Anything?" Bobby raised his voice and one of the workers came out on the porch.

Sophia looked up when the clerked asked if everything was alright. "Yes, it is fine. You can go back in. I am okay."

Then Sophia stood up and walked out into the yard and sat down by the big Oak tree. Bobby followed her. He stood some distance so he could see her face. Sophia began to speak. "I know you thought that Maggie and Katlynn should have stayed here, but Maggie always hated it here. And what kind of life would Katlynn have now if she had stayed. I know we disagree about this. Our disagreement is caused by different perceptions."

Bobby cleared his throat. "Sophia, perception is based on opinion. And my opinion is that we should have been there for Maggie and Katlynn. She needed a man, a daddy figure in her life. We could have been that for her. Life is all about perception. Positive versus negative. Whichever you choose will affect and more likely reflect your outcomes. You denied us that opportunity to be there for them. And they did not even have a choice because you made it for them."

Sophia stood up. "I perceived that they were better off in Wake Forest. Maggie took a job she loved and Katlynn went on to be successful. And that is the truth."

Bobby squared his shoulders. "Trust takes years to build, Sophia, and seconds to break. It will be forever to repair."

Sophia took a step toward him. "Can we disagree while trying to remain respectful? Can we do that for Katlynn, if not for us? I still feel I was right, but after seeing her this week maybe, just maybe I should have let her visit in the summer. I guess I was afraid she and Maggie would leave and not come back."

Bobby turned to walk away. "So, the real issue was that you were afraid of losing them. Now the truth comes out."

Bobby saw Katlynn looking out the third story window. He waved and smiled, got into his truck and rode away.

When Maggie and she went out to the porch Sophia was sitting where they left her. She never said a word about Bobby and Katlynn did not ask. Maybe Damian was right. Sometimes things do not turn out like you thought they would be. They rode back to the RV and had a cookout with the rest of team. By the fire in the late evening Katlynn reflected while everyone was talking and laughing. Sometimes you have to forget what is gone and appreciate what remains and look forward to what is coming next.

Chapter 16

It was good to go to Harkers Island, but it was better to be back home. She had missed Damian. When she returned, he was not in the apartment. She found him in the library at a table, papers all around him. He looked like a student instead of a professor. Katlynn sneaked up behind him and put her hands over his eyes. "Guess who?"

He took her hands off his eyes and turned around. He kissed her hard and some students giggled. She helped him gather his papers and they went outside to a picnic table. The sun glistened in her hair and Damian thought how beautiful she was. He was glad she was investigating something totally different than her chosen career, but was glad she was home.

She had won so many trophies and awards as a journalist. She had motivated people under her supervision to dream big or go home. Katlynn had a way about her that drew people to her and drew them to do their best for her. He had always had a passion for education and was taking classes for years to get his PhD to teach. Now he was teaching and loving it. The research part of being a professor was difficult and challenging at times, but he found his passion. He just hoped that he had not squashed Katlynn's by asking her to follow him back to North Carolina to pursue his dream.

Damian put his elbows on the table, his chin on his hands. He looked at every facial feature of Katlynn. He looked into her eyes trying to see something. Was she as happy as he was? He did not want her to lose herself. He did not want her unhappy and unfulfilled. It was a balance that married people had to make.

Katlynn leaned into the table and looked at him. "It looks like you are in deep thought. What is it? Is everything okay?"

Damian spoke softly. "I hope so. While I was busy pursuing my dreams and found myself in this place with this opportunity, I had not thought how it would affect you and us. I feel fulfilled and content and with a purpose; not that my other job as a journalist was not meaningful. I didn't mean it

174

that way. I just feel that I am making a difference in the world by being here and teaching. Does this make sense to you?"

Katlynn's face softened. "Yes, it does make sense. Working hard for something we love is called passion. I had a passion for journalism and went after it with all my might. After my heart attack I had a lot of time to reevaluate my life. I never would have thought I would end up here again. You know, where I started. I just need time to find out what it is I am supposed to be and do."

The evening sun was setting. They gathered their things and headed back to the apartment. Life has a way of moving on; you go to work to make a living, come home, eat, sleep and do it all over again. And if you are one of the lucky ones you have work that fulfills you and makes a difference in the lives of others as well. They tried to see Maggie and Aunt Sophia at least twice a month; Damian's work took a lot of his time as well as Katlynn's as they entertained students sometimes at their home. That was all part of building relationships; a part of his job, too. She enjoyed that part as well.

Katlynn attended one of Damian's classes again. The students were to get up in front of the class and recite their own poetry. The one she liked best was by a girl named Vivian. It went like this.

Life is too short to wake up in the morning with regrets.

So, love the people who treat you right and forgive the ones who do not.

And believe everything happens for a reason.

If you are lucky enough to get a chance- take it.

If it changes your life- let it.

Nobody said it would be easy.

They just promised it would be worth it.

How true, thought Katlynn. She no longer wanted to wake up with regrets. She wanted to live intentional. Life is too short to not forgive and to move on. Hold no grudges and let go of what would have been. She did believe that everything happens for a reason. She just had not found out what that reason was yet, but she would know when it happened. If anything from her heart attack she had learned it was to wait and be still. And she was waiting for the next chance that would come along soon. She felt it in her bones. And when that chance would come, she would embrace it. Her journey had not been easy, but whatever was next would be worth it.

The environmental science class this week was about farming. Farming in North Carolina lends lots of opportunities depending on which region you are in. Katlynn learned that crops such as tobacco, soybeans, corn, cotton, sweet potatoes, hay, peanuts, wheat, blueberries, apples, tomatoes, strawberries, melons, cucumbers, peppers, squash, beans, cabbage, grapes and peaches were huge crops for the state. There is a lot of certifications, inspections, compliance and regulatory rules for land farmers. Katlynn had no idea before this class how much went in to food for her to eat. She had a much more appreciation.

Then she learned also that sometimes the weather has a bearing on crops; it is not unusual for droughts or flooding to wipe out crops and leave the land farmer without food and money for their families. She learned about North Carolina's Disaster Assistance Program. There were programs for farm land damage and crop losses. There were also programs to help with emergency loans. This all fascinated Katlynn. She came home and talked to Damian about her day and what she learned.

Damian listened. "It gives me a more appreciation for who grows our food we eat. Is there any assistance for commercial fisherman and shrimpers?"

"No," Katlynn said. "I asked that question. The professor said that fishermen do not own the sea. So, at this time there is nothing for them. I remember hearing mama and daddy talking, keeping their voices low as to not awaken me. But I could hear daddy tell mama that they had not caught enough shrimp to make money last the rest of the year. Mama said she would just keep working her waitress job. He kept promising her next year would be different. And she begged him to go back to Wake Forest and Raleigh area, but he could not leave, he said. And some years he made a lot of money and mama could have stopped working. She was afraid not to work; afraid of the uncertainty. Daddy told her once that uncertainty is life's way of saying that there are only a few things you can control. And uncertainty is a pathway to growth, he used to say. She said she did not buy that."

The next several months' life went on as usual. It was nearing the end of the academic year and heading towards graduation. Damian was consumed with grading and preparing for this big event which left Katlynn time alone. She went into journalism mode and started researching everything she could find on legislation and politics about commercial farming and the fishing industry. She had a notebook filled with notes and lots of questions. One of the questions was how do crew members of a fishing boat get paid. She learned that the crew members signed a contract at the beginning of each season with the owner of the boat. They are usually paid a percentage of the catch minus their share of certain expenses (food bill, insurance, fuel). They get a paycheck at the end of the season less any advances they might have asked for during the season. The check comes from the captain. They get their full paycheck and no taxes are removed so they need to be sure to save enough to pay them come tax time. This, thought Katlynn, would be very difficult to manage a budget on. She did not know if they could do it.

The next question was how the pay process worked for the boat captain. She learned that if you're the license owner your permit is what allows you to sell your catch. It may also have restrictions around how you sell it. Many fishermen sell their catch to processors. The catch is weighed and the weights are recorded on an invoice. Once all the weights have been taken the processors agent takes a carbon copy of your license card and both the license holder and the processors agent sign the invoice. Each get a copy. The invoices are compiled and tracked for each license holder. At the end of the season the processor will cut each license holder who delivers to them a check for the season's fish. The license holder has to do all their own accounting for crew shares and boat expenses. This is just a gross payment.

179

Wow, thought Katlynn again. No wonder this was so hard for daddy and his crew to plan and manage. They had no control of how much shrimp they caught. And immediately and some years after a hurricane it affected sea life.

After Hurricane Florence Katlynn learned that the pollution from flooding in cities eventually ended up in the Cape Fear and Neuse River, then in Pamlico Sound, and finally in the Atlantic Ocean which made seafood unsafe to eat. The commercial fishermen in Carteret County and others then had to contend with harvesting of clams, mussels, oysters and shrimping being forbidden by the state agency. This undoubtedly hurt the economics of the seafood industry in the county, but the risk to human health was most considered. But with most areas Down East getting 8 feet of water it was more than enough to mess up the ecosystem of shellfish, crabs, and shrimp. It was a complex problem; one that kept her up at night.

At three o'clock in the morning Damian rolled over and found Katlynn gone again. She had been doing that quite a lot lately. He found her on their front stoop with a cup of hot tea in her hand sitting on the chair.

"What are you doing? Do you know what time it is?" Damian asked softly and compassionately.

"I cannot sleep." Katlynn said as she yawned.

"I can see that. But why are you not sleeping? What is bothering you, Katlynn?" Damian sat on the ground at her feet and looked up at her.

"I cannot help thinking about all the research that I have done on commercial fishermen and how this last hurricane has devastated these families. It is like they are a casualty of war. I am a product of it; I feel their pain. It looks like I could do something or someone could do something. But what? I am losing sleep over this." Katlynn yawned again.

"You are passionate about this, Katlynn. Come on to bed. What I found out a long time ago was that your passion would lead you right into your purpose. Doors will open for you soon, honey. Get some sleep so you will be ready for the next thing." Damian stood up and took her hand and pulled her up from the chair. He carried her to bed. Her head hit the pillow and she was gone fast asleep.

Graduation day came. It was fun to see all the professors in their gowns march in after the students had been seated. Katlynn winked at Damian as he walked by. At the end of the ceremony hats whirled skyward, carried by bright new hopes and propelled by big daring dreams. The speaker had ended her speech by a quote from Gabrielle Bernstein. "Allow your passion to become your purpose. It will one day become your profession." Katlynn felt her heart shudder. Was she talking directly to her?

The speaker must have been talking directly to her because doors began to open for Katlynn. She and Damian were invited to a dinner party. Republican State House Representative Pat McElraft was there. Katlynn told her about her life as a child in Harkers Island, her journey to New York and her journey back to North Carolina. She told her of the interviews and research she had done about commercial fishing; especially her passion for shrimpers. She listened intently and went back to Raleigh. She and many others worked on an assistance program to help commercial fishermen Down East with their losses.

The assistance program approved was through the "Trip Ticket" program administered by the Division of Marine Fisheries which allows for a verification process by looking at an average of the past few years landings and comparing it to the affected months in 2018. Not only does this effort help families, but also assures that the taxpayers are helping those that can verify their losses. Katlynn was even able to interview

Republican State House Representative Pat McElraft and received permission to quote her.

"It was very important to understand the losses incurred by land farmers and also our farmers of the sea. Farm families were awarded almost $250M for recovery including the $11.6M given to the commercial fishermen out of the state's Rainy-Day fund. It is also important to get our tourism industry up and running again. I'll be working on getting some advertising money to let the public know the Crystal Coast is back in business." says Republican State House Representative Pat McElraft when asked about the assistance.

When the article came out in local newspapers Katlynn was proud of the story and the awareness it brought. She had found the beginning of her passion. Would another door open for her? That answer would be a yes. Soon after Damian and Katlynn were asked to attend another function. There she met retired Professor Tilley again. He recognized her immediately and came over to her. He placed an envelope in her hand and said, "I do not stick my reputation out for just anyone, Mrs. Davito, so take this opportunity and fill out this application. Good luck. I will put in a word for you." Then he walked away. Katlynn put it in her purse; she would look at it in the quietness of her home.

Once they were home, she pulled it out and opened it. It was an application for the job with the government in Raleigh, North Carolina at the Capitol Building overseeing the North Carolina Environmental Quality department. The one that her daddy had held for a short time. She placed it over her heart and began to weep. Damian came into the room and asked her what was wrong.

"Nothing," she said. "Absolutely nothing. I have found my passion and if I am honored and chosen it will be my profession." She then told him all about it. She filled out the application with a cover letter and put it in the mail. She could have done it online, but she wanted to honor Professor Tilley. He had earned respect and she wanted to honor that as well.

Katlynn interviewed and was offered the job. The first day at the office she was greeted and welcomed by everyone; but especially those who had worked for a short time with Jim Harcourt. Her office was small; a room 8' x 8'.

There was a small desk, two bookcases and file cabinets that lined another wall. The only chair in the office was her swivel chair.

A conference room was right next door if she had to meet with anyone. There was one small window. How unlike her New York office. But she was comfortable and had a peace about it. She looked around the room and found only one empty spot on the wall.

Her Administrative Assistant, Holly, stood at the door. "Welcome. The last person who had this job put his diploma on the wall in that spot." Holly had a hammer and a nail in her hand.

Katlynn took it from her. "I know the perfect picture for this spot."

She carefully unwrapped the picture of her and her daddy on the shrimping boat, put a nail in the wall and hung it. She stepped back to look at it. Holly nodded in approval.

Katlynn looked at Holly and said, "Someone once told me that life takes you to unexpected places, but love brings you home."

The phone rang. Katlynn went immediately to work.